York Ferry

York Ferry

Annie Dawid

CANE HILL PRESS

Library of Congress Catalog Number 92-53146
Copyright © 1993 by Annie Dawid
All rights reserved
Printed in the United States of America
    First edition
    ISBN No. 0-943433-10-X
Cover photograph by Annie Dawid

Portions of this book have appeared, in slightly different form, in *The Dickinson Review* (1987), *The Gettysburg Review* (1989), *The Northern Review* (1989), *North Country* (1990), *Blueline* (1990, 1991, 1992), *Eclectic Literary Forum* (1991), *Salmon* (1992), and *Women on Women II* (1993).

Permission for lyrics from "The M.T.A." granted by Atlantic Music Corp. (1956).

Published by
Cane Hill Press
225 Varick Street
New York, NY 10014

 Produced at The Print Center., Inc., 225 Varick St., New York, NY 10014, a non-profit facility for literary and arts-related publications. (212) 206-8465

"Love's mysteries in souls do grow."
John Donne

For Michael Rubin
(1935-1989)

Teacher, Mentor, Friend

Chapter One

1960

While her daughter, Zoe Mae, investigated some overgrown phlox at the edge of the platform, Kay Pinny waited for the rumble in the air, the wheeze of the black engine car to signal the arrival of the New York-Montreal passenger train. Clutching her straw bag in one hand, Vernon's red bandanna in the other, she anticipated the engineer's surprise at the sight of a small woman in white with white hair and a shockingly redheaded child at a station where few boarded at this time of year. A flag stop. It was rare, too, that a York Ferry year-round resident would await the train for her own transportation; local people at the depot were usually there in service to the wealthy families who owned property along the lakeshore, whose spacious homes sat boarded up all winter. In the still brisk morning, no one else was there. Kay's oldest son, Dean, had volunteered to wait with them, but she insisted he go to school, as if nothing had happened. She drove over in the pickup because her Buick had broken down the Friday before with something minor—a blown gasket or plug, her husband said—but here it was Wednesday, and her LeSabre remained unmoving behind the farmhouse, Vernon's promise to fix it frozen like cirrus in the crisp Adirondack air.

Her watch read somewhere between 8:15 and 8:30. She couldn't tell exactly because of the fogged glass on the lower right-hand side. On her first day wearing the Timex—a birthday

1

present from Vernon and the children—she'd washed a load of breakfast dishes and then put her hands in the dirt to plant sunflowers, seeding a row to frame the farmhouse. From where he sat on the porch holding Zoe Mae, Vernon saw the glass glinting on her wrist.

"Oh, Mrs. Pinny!" he called, using her formal name to indicate he had something official to say. "That watch we bought you doesn't go underwater. Or underground, I guess. The salesman said to tell you. Maybe I forgot."

The watch continued to tick, though, losing five minutes in the morning, gaining them back at night, its hands faithfully whirling beneath the patch of fog that never went away.

Under her feet, the ground began to pulse. Kay called Zoe Mae and held her hand while waving the red kerchief like a semaphore, steady and regular, even before the train showed itself. Kay liked the vibrations traveling upward through her body from the soles of her feet, liked to imagine the train connected to some deep vein in the earth, railroad tracks like arteries linking all the crucial places. Holding her daughter even tighter when the huge engine car appeared from the south, shooting from a shadowy break in the pines, Kay continued to wave the bandanna, hoping she was flagging properly. The long silver cars wriggled like centipede segments, slowing and straightening until the last one stopped with its doorway directly in front of them.

A set of metal steps unhinged, and a man in blue descended. "Good morning. Traveling light today, are you? Is this all you have?" he asked, picking up Kay's shopping bag full of fruit and sandwiches before lifting her daughter up and onto the train.

It's far from all, she thought. How much does one disclose to a railway conductor? She wanted to tell him that her husband had run away, but it sounded almost silly; it was something one said about small children. They ran away; they came back. But Kay had the disquieting feeling that Vernon had no intention of coming back. "That's it. That's all," she said, accepting his capable old hand to assist her up the stairs.

"We don't often have folks getting on here," he said, steering her toward an empty set of seats as the train picked up speed, which made her weave crazily down the aisle. "Not this early in the season, anyway."

Kay was smiling in spite of all that had propelled her to take a train for the first time in her life. Feeling the rumbling ground had excited her, but this was even better: the land slipping away beneath the wheels, the shaking back and forth as the rails disappeared behind them, the soothing, steady clack of travel.

Well did he ever return, no he never returned
and his fate is still unlearned.
He may ride forever 'neath the streets of Boston.
He's the man
who never returned.

Lines from a song she'd heard Dean sing flitted across her memory. For a moment, she wanted to run away herself, to ride on and on, away from responsibility and ordinariness. But Kay had never considered herself the fleeing kind; leaving her home was an adventure only because she would return.

"Where are you going this morning, Ma'am?" The conductor deposited the bag overhead, Zoe Mae in the window seat, and leafed through a ticketbook as thick as a dictionary. "Port Elizabeth? Plattsburgh?"

"Montreal, please." In all her forty years, Kay had never spoken a word with such intensity, as if pronouncing her destination correctly would help clarify her reasons for going.

The conductor raised his formidable eyebrows, which reminded her of scrub brush bristles. "Two for Montreal, then. How old's the girl?"

"Three."

"She rides free, then. That'll be five dollars one way, twice that round trip."

It was more than Kay had predicted. Biting her lower lip, she counted out ten dollar bills and let Zoe Mae hold the ticket stubs after the conductor delighted her by creating a handful of colored confetti with his puncher. Wide-eyed, she pointed at everything they passed, demanding her mother's attention in a loud and cheerful voice.

"Look! There's the lake!" she cried, pressing her palm into the glass as if she were trying to capture in her stubby, freckled fingers the blue mists over Lake Champlain. York Ferry occupied a minuscule three miles of coast on the huge lake, which stretched south from Canada for over a hundred miles. The village passed by in a whir: supermarket, hardware store, two bars, gas station, two churches, and the low metal bridge, painted green, crossing the Bouquet River, pronounced *Bo-KET*.

"Who lives there?" Zoe Mae asked as they whisked by a decrepit wooden shack in a field brimming with weeds, an old cow pasture gone to seed.

"No one, I guess. Maybe some animals. A black bear. I bet a carefree mother bear lives there," said Kay, who was trying to imagine how she would go about telling her five children that their father was gone, that he'd deserted them for some obscure reason she herself had difficulty understanding. The letter that arrived the day before bore the address of a Montreal hotel; she was sure he would already have gone, and Kay and her daughter would simply about-face and go home. But she had to look for him, even though she believed their journey futile from the beginning, had to explore the most remote possibility Vernon might be rescued. Maybe their youngest child could charm him back, or jolt him to his senses, or merely make him feel guilty enough to reconsider. Vernon was a stubborn man, though, and rarely changed his mind once an opinion was set. Kay wondered if stubbornness was the same as pride, going before the fall. Frowning, she chided herself for thinking like her mother, who found an answer for everything in the "great, good book."

Kay removed the letter from her straw pocketbook and read it again, for perhaps the twentieth time since she'd taken it from the mailbox at the foot of their dirt driveway, along with a circular advertising the new Sears in Plattsburgh. Vernon's handwriting was small and careful, i's all dotted, t's crossed, written in lines so straight she supposed he'd used a ruler, or one of those guides that came with thin stationery. The only thing wrong, which made the whole letter look peculiar, was that the sentences went all the way from one side of the page to the other, without an attempt at a margin. Some of the words fell off the edges, disappearing midway, even in the middle of a letter.

L'Hotel Saule Pleureur
Rue de beaux arbres, 12
Montréal, Quebec

June 12, 1960

Dear Kay:

I can't hardly explain why I left, but now that I have, I know I can't come back. At least not for a while. Once you start a thing, it's hard to change directions—momentum takes hold, or something like that. I thought it would be like Europe here, like the Belgium I remember from 1944, but it's not. The people talk so strange—doesn't even sound like French. More like Texan. I'm thinking I'll go see Antwerp again, look for Irene, the girl I told you about, from long before you and I got married. Look for her grave, I mean. I never looked at anyone else, Kay, or drank too much or threw money away. My conscience tells me I've been a good husband to you—up till now, that is. But I need to go. I have to go. Now seems like the right time—the mortgage is paid, and Henry can run the shop. (I trained him pretty well, and business has picked up lately.) I'll send money whenever I can. And I know I can't ask this without being a hypocrite, but I will anyway because I can't help it: will you wait for me? Wait until I write you what's happened. I guess you'll do what you see fit—you always do— and the wife of a man who's left his family is bound to have everyone on her side if she does find someone else, but just wait a little. Wait a year. Please. I don't know what you should tell the children. That part I just can't figure out. You'll think of something, Kay. I know you will.

Your,
Vernon

"How come the boys didn't get to come?"

"Well, Dean and Steve had school, and Grandma said she'd stay home with the twins. So it's just you and me, pumpkin." She patted her daughter's head, the fire-colored hair exploding in curls despite the two careful braids Kay had made earlier, trying to impose order on the chaotic mass of frizz. "Why don't you try and nap a little?" Of course, suggesting it had been the wrong tack; Kay knew as soon as the words were out. Zoe Mae, her only girl, was already as stubborn as her father. Although she'd barely been able to keep her eyes open, Zoe Mae would now make a valiant effort to stay awake as long as possible.

When the train stopped at Plattsburgh for a few minutes, they stepped out to buy something from a man selling drinks behind a small cart. He looked about the same age as Vernon, who was three years younger than Kay; he wore a flag pin with the words "Disabled Veteran of World War II" on his shirt pocket; a medal hung from a faded lavender ribbon. His thick sunglasses, conspicuous in the still cloudy morning, indicated his blindness, but Zoe Mae didn't understand their use.

"Can I get you some juice, Ma'am? Or how about some milk for your daughter?" he asked before Kay had spoken. Perhaps the sound of her heels hitting the pavement had alerted him, as well as the scuffling of Zoe Mae's stiff Mary Janes, which she tried to use as skates across the platform.

"Some milk, sweetie?"

"Okay." Zoe Mae raised her arms to be lifted up to adult level, and her mother obliged.

"Here, give the man a quarter," said Kay loudly, pressing the coin into her daughter's plump fist. "Go ahead." She lowered her voice as Zoe Mae gazed at the man's face quizzically, and then at her mother, and then back again.

"Why are you wearing sunglasses? The sun's not out yet."

"Please forgive her," Kay said, her face burning, but the man dismissed her words with a snap of his wrist, as if to flick away a bothersome fly.

"It's a natural question for a curious little girl," he said. "I'll tell her. I wear these glasses because I can't see. Now, I know that doesn't make any sense, but I'm told my eyes are so hideous, so damn horrible to look at that I have to cover them up so no one else can see them. It's like they're glasses for everyone but me." He fingered his medal. "They look at this, though."

"Can I see your eyes?" asked Zoe Mae immediately.

"Zoe Mae!" Kay snapped.

Just then the train whistle blew, and the conductor yelled, "All aboard for Mon-tree-all. All aboard!" She mumbled her thanks to the veteran, whose forefinger and thumb still rested on the rim of his dark glasses, poised to bare his ugliness to Zoe Mae.

Kay rushed up the stairs carrying her daughter, who resisted by going completely limp, her body a solid, heavy mass. "Why couldn't I see them?" Zoe Mae was not content with her mother's determined head-shaking. "Why? Why couldn't I?"

Sighing, Kay pictured Zoe Mae's life unfurling as an endless wave of unanswerable questions, her curiosity continuing unabated through old age. Her bright hair might fade, her freckles wash away, but still she would ask *why*, her green eyes lit with the hope that comes from believing in answers, trusting that all you need to do is ask the right question and enlightenment will follow. Zoe Mae was just like Dean had been at that age, able to play the why game for hours and hours. "Why didn't the sun come out today? Why can't you see it if it's there? Why doesn't it change sizes like the moon?" Kay and Vernon had marveled at the extent of Dean's inquisitiveness and were often stumped, their backgrounds inadequate to the task of answering their child's questions. Kay didn't know what clouds were made of, or why the mountains had settled in the shapes they had, why the westernmost range they could see from their porch looked like a sleeping woman. It just did, and Kay refused to tell her children that God had made it that way, as her mother had told her, attributing everything she couldn't explain to God's ultimate wisdom. Kay didn't believe in God. During the war, when all the men her age failed to return to York Ferry, Kay stopped subscribing to her mother's traditional faith and belief in God the Father. Kay's answers to her children often lacked authority—a deficiency of which she was well aware—but she preferred confessing ignorance to lying. The blind man had been unkind to force his sorrows on her little girl; why would seeing his dead eyes help Zoe Mae understand the man's misery? Kay wished they had stayed on the train and remained thirsty.

A car lot just north of the city drew her daughter's attention, red and green sedans, an array of gleaming new Buicks, glistening beneath the hose of a proprietor preparing for the day, the lot looking like an early Christmas display. Zoe Mae waved; she had already left the blind man's eyes behind.

The rock and lull of the train enticed Kay into a light sleep north of the city, where the land turned to farms again, to green open pasture spotted with dairy cows. When the sun's rays finally perforated the fog, the dewy surface of the countryside turned silver. Now the Adirondacks were gilded and the sun was everywhere, risen above Vermont's Green Mountains to the east, flooding the stippled waters of Lake Champlain that divided the two states like a heart. Gulls flapped beside the windows as the train followed the shore, sailboats and the occasional ferry flashing into view as in a filmstrip, then disappearing, replaced with the deep rich blue of the endless water. Zoe Mae fell asleep, too, the ticket stubs dropping from her fist to the floor and slipping across it, coming to rest underneath the seat behind them. For miles, heading inland, one could see nothing but occasional farm buildings encircled by acres and acres of cornfields. The whistle sounded purposefully as the train sped onward, crossing dirt roads unadorned by flashing lights or warning barriers, slowing over the fragile bridges, startling a great blue heron bathing in a stream, who took sudden flight and soared high above the train, the narrow cars pushing north and north, like blood racing toward the extremities; and the heron returned to its bath, settling its wings into a leisure that would be broken only by the next racing train. The passengers slept through the empty miles, and the train came finally to a halt at the Canadian border.

Kay and her daughter awoke simultaneously, smiling at one another under lashes fluttering with crusted sleep, dreams elusive fragments. When Kay handed their birth certificates to a uniformed border guard, she listened carefully to his accent, trying to understand her husband's displeasure. The man's voice was nasal with an odd twang to it, but easy enough to comprehend.

"And how long are you staying in Canada, Madam?"

She liked being called madam. "Just today, I think. Maybe tomorrow, depending."

"And do you have a particular destination? Or are you visiting as a tourist?"

Kay showed him the embossed return address on Vernon's envelope. The man inspected it, shrugged, and said, "Very good, then. Have a pleasant stay in Canada." He bowed slightly, then went on to the next passenger.

"Why did he have to see those papers?"

"We're in another country now, sweetie. They have a different language here. And different laws." Kay spoke vaguely, since she had never traveled to a foreign country before, not even to Canada, which had always been this close. She couldn't say why, exactly. Her parents had spent their honeymoon in the Canadian Thousand Islands but had never again crossed the border. Their own country was good enough, thank you, they said; they had no need of foreign lands in which to take their vacations.

As they approached downtown Montreal, the city rose up around them brushing the sky, like enormous building blocks grown all out of proportion, a giant's playthings. Her heart beat rapidly as they crossed high above the Saint Lawrence River, quicker and quicker as the train slowed to a crawl outside Central Station. She didn't know how frightened she was until all the passengers had left, and she still sat, clutching her daughter's dappled hand, afraid to move for fear of something huge and dangerous appearing out of the foreign skies to devour them as soon as they stepped outside. The train's interior was so cozy compared to the vastness on the other side of the window.

"What are we waiting for?" Zoe Mae asked, anxious to be out in the sun, which dazzled both of them now, hitting the roof of a train across the platform, striking the cement so that millions of mica diamonds glittered all the way to the depot building, where what looked to Kay like thousands of people dressed in suits and elegant dresses bustled in and out of the perpetually opening doors.

"We're waiting for your old mother to get her courage up, that's what." Kay laughed nervously and adjusted her hair, which was pinned in a crown of braids above her ears. She hoped that her clothing—an egg-white suit and pale yellow blouse—wasn't too shabby, too out-of-date, a signal to the citizens of Montreal that she was a hick, a woman easily tricked by cabbies and shopkeeps.

Out on the street, Kay's fears dissolved in the din of the metropolitan morning. "It's kind of exciting, isn't it?" she asked her daughter, who agreed but demanded to be picked up out of the way of the marching pairs of legs, briefcases, and suitcases bouncing all around her. It was impossible to hold Zoe Mae, the bag, and her purse all at once, so Kay pleaded with her to hold tight to her skirt as they made their way to a cab stand, which was what Kay's mother had advised her to do.

"Just take out the address and point to it," Eleanor had said early that morning as they sipped coffee together at the farmhouse. Eleanor hadn't been very sympathetic since Vernon's disappearance; she seemed to be gloating that she had known all along her son-in-law was a bad seed, that it would come to this eventually. "That way you won't have any misunderstanding, 'cause you can't figure out that Frog they speak, even when they're talking English."

Huddled in an oversized yellow cab, Kay handed the driver Vernon's envelope. The short gray hair poking out from beneath the cabbie's cap turned out to belong to an older woman, heavy-set and gruff. "Lady, that's a really long ride. It'll be a lot of money. If I were you, I'd take that trolley over there and get off at the last stop. Just tell the conductor you want the Rude Bazaar. Cost you only a quarter that way." Her gaze met Kay's in the rear-view mirror. "I mean, I'll take you there," she said, her voice softening, "but it won't even be a whole lot faster." Then the woman smiled, very kindly, Kay thought. She felt disappointed, though, that the driver had figured out Kay didn't belong.

"I guess we'll take the trolley, then. Thank you, Madam. Thanks very much."

"Sure thing." The older woman tipped her cap.

Kay was impressed by the driver, who found another passenger as soon as Kay and Zoe Mae left the car.

They found their way to the Hotel Saule Pleureur without getting lost, a minor miracle to Kay. The Rude Bazaar turned out to be the name of the street. Zoe Mae adored the ride, leaning out the window the whole time, her braids flapping. Green weeping willows draped the street and its stately old buildings, reminding Kay of the Lakeshore Drive at home. She understood why Vernon had chosen this place. Before they went into the hotel office, she crouched down to tell Zoe Mae, after smoothing the girl's unruly hair and adjusting her sailor dress, "Now, don't ask Daddy why he's been gone—if we find him here, that is—okay? I'll do that."

"But why *has* he been gone?"

"I'm not sure, Zoe Mae," Kay whispered. "That's what we're going to find out."

Kay began to sweat immediately upon opening the door. A woman appeared and asked her a question in a mysterious blur of sound. Kay felt positive he wasn't there.

"Monsieur Pinny?" the woman said, accenting the second syl-

11

lable instead of the first. "No, he is gone this morning, already a few hours."

Kay rested her hands on the reception desk for balance; her legs wobbled. Although she knew this already, although she thought she'd known exactly what was coming—people always remarked how sensible she was—Kay felt dizzy, her knees as weak as when she took her first step out of anesthesia after Dean was born.

The woman scurried over to help her to a chair. Then she brought a glass of water and wrung her hands, looking anxiously from mother to daughter to the door. "Is something wrong? Was he to wait for you?"

"I thought he might."

"This is the daughter, no? I can see him in her face."

Kay closed her eyes and cried for a while, stubborn tears pushing out from the corners of her eyes and settling into her prematurely white hair as she sat in the plain, strange room, her head turned toward the ceiling, where a wooden fan circulated the rapidly warming air, while her daughter, baffled, kept asking, "Where is he? Why isn't he here? Why are you crying?" And Zoe Mae's why's filled the room, tumbling out the windows and doors, jamming the sky with questions.

1961

Vancouver, British Columbia
Dec. 24

Dear Kay,

You've probably given me up for dead by now, but I'm still here, still in Canada, although I hadn't meant to be. I didn't have enough money to get on a boat or plane for Europe, so I took a job working on train engines for Canadian National. They've been moving me all over this country, which is huge. Forests go on forever. And the mountains we crossed to get here, the Canadian Rockies—you've never seen anything like them in your life, Kay. Like ice they are, enormous slabs of ice, miles high—like when the lake starts breaking up in spring. I remember the roaring sound of the thaw when the Champlain starts moving again. That's the music I had playing in my head as we crossed over, the train and me such puny ants belly-crawling through a frozen heaven. Here's my Christmas bonus, and another $200. I'm sorry it's not more.

Are you still waiting for me? How are the children? You can write me here, general delivery, and send some pictures. I always took all the pictures, didn't I? But I suppose you've learned to use the camera now. Please send me snapshots. I'm hungry to see how the kids are doing, and I forgot to pack any photos when I left. I'm still trying to figure out what to do, and I haven't made up my mind. That's why I didn't write earlier. But I finally decided that you'd probably want to know I was at least alive. I haven't been with anyone. I think about you a lot. The farmhouse. York Ferry. My parents' graves in the cemetery under that lightning-struck oak. It still hurts that they died while I was overseas. I think about Irene, dead at 20. She had the bluest eyes, like the lake in summer at dawn. It was hard to believe she was a Jew with those eyes. Irene Stein. Of course you don't pronounce Irene like we do—it sounded more like eee-wren. Like the bird. But here I am talking about her when I meant to give you some kind of explanation. I'm sorry.

I wrote to wish you a Merry Christmas, to wish you two, really, since I missed last year's. I hope you'll forgive me.

Vernon

1963

Skagway, Alaska
April 1

Dear Kay,

I wonder how I got here, back in the United States, when I meant to leave for Europe. It's the trains, I guess. I'm working on a narrow-gauge rail up to the Yukon, mostly repairing, though sometimes I run them if need be. It's so remote up here—I like it. I like the trains better than autos and trucks and planes—all those engines I had my hands in for so many years. The planes remind me too much of the war, and the others too much of York Ferry, I guess. There's something so huge about the trains, so grand. Bigger than life they are, bigger than you could imagine from seeing them in the movies. I know you've never been on a train. Once we talked about doing that, didn't we? Taking a train south to see the Gulf of Mexico and New Orleans. Or was that my idea? Why didn't we ever go?

Why don't you write me, Kay? Send me a picture, at least. I know that what I did was wrong. It seems I keep making the wrong decisions—and the important ones I foul up the worst. But I can't undo them, can I? Not Irene—I can't undo that—and not June 12th either. If or when I come back, it's not the same as undoing. It doesn't erase what I did or change what happened. I thought you'd write to say how angry you were. I hoped you'd say you were mad but you still wanted me back, still cared in some way, but you don't write anything at all.

Sometimes I wonder if we shouldn't have gotten married, even though of course I love our children. Both of us were so lonely—friends who came together at a convenient time. In 1945 there weren't many men of marriageable age in York Ferry. And you said yourself you were getting old, especially considering you wanted to have a little girl. All that work I did on your Ford's clutch, all those afternoons of our courtship in the York Ferry Garage, me covered in grease, you in blood from the butcher shop. I did love you, Kay. But I was *in love* during the war. I guess I still am in love with that Belgian girl I met in 1944. I want to go find her grave and apologize for not rescuing her. For three years she'd hidden in a room with no windows, and after the Brits finally opened up Antwerp, she went outside for the first time. Can you imagine what that air must have felt like? I met her when we started using the port to supply our troops in the east. Then I was out in the Bastogne, which we captured, god damn it, and when I got back to Antwerp I found she'd gotten hit by one of those V-2s the Germans were pelting the city with. It makes me sick how far those bombs could travel.

Maybe she doesn't have a grave. I was so numb when I found out, I didn't know what I was doing. When I write you again, I plan to be able to tell you what the hell I'm doing. Maybe I'll tell you that I'm coming home. Here's $400, which I've been saving for you. What have you told the kids about me? I think about them all the time, though you may not believe that—especially the last boy. I bet the girl can hardly remember me.

I'm still waiting on those pictures. Please write me here, general delivery. As soon as I get enough money together, I'll get down to Seattle and board a plane to Belgium, get this out of my system or something. I swear I care for you, Kay. I just need some more time to get this all figured out.

Vernon

Chapter Two

1964

Snow drifted down outside, and the farmhouse was warm and snug against the cold, a cozy refuge, Kay thought, from the chaos beyond their valley. Zoe Mae chattered beside Eleanor, Kay's mother, who was carrying the turkey platter at chest level, taking careful, steady steps. Dinner was ready. Kay sniffed the air, content, and smiled around the table at her family: the twins at the far end; Dean on her right (she was sitting at the head, in Vernon's old place); beside him Steve, her next boy. To her left was Zoe Mae, then Eleanor. Kay had cooked most of the night and morning with the agreement that her mother would serve and the older boys clean up. The smell of butter and onions and gravy permeated the kitchen, and yeast, too, from the bread she only had time to bake on holidays. She breathed in the sweet syrupiness of candied yams with marshmallows, apple pie and cinnamon. The kitchen counters brimmed with the fruits of her own harvest, the bountiful yield of the vegetable garden. Kay loved Thanksgiving more than any holiday; Christmas made her nervous. She was never sure if she'd bought the right presents, and always knew she hadn't bought enough; Christmas called for the man bearing gifts, and there was none. At Thanksgiving, the family spent the day eating and resting and eating again, sitting by the woodstove and playing board games, walking down to the lake for a digestive stroll when the weather permitted, and staying home at night. It was tradition, a ritual Kay never wanted to change.

But this year might be the last Pinny-only dinner, because Dean would probably want to bring a girl friend next Thanksgiving. Yesterday he'd asked somewhat tentatively, "What would you think if I invited Cathy Reiser to dinner?" Kay, daring selfishness, said she'd rather he didn't, just this last time. Dean's response was an enigmatic shrug.

"Kayleen, do we have everything?" her mother asked, resting her hands in the pockets of her apron, an orange and blue flowered print that covered her severe Sunday dress.

Kay surveyed the table. All the condiments were there: cranberry relish, butter, two gravy boats, salt and pepper, extra napkins. "Mother, I think we've got it. Sit down, please."

Eleanor took off the apron and draped it over her chair. All six faces turned toward Kay expectantly.

There they all were: her five children, her mother, and the shepherd mutt, Herkimer, his head on her feet beneath the tablecloth. She raised her glass with its few drops of Champagne (another tradition) and said, "Mother, Dean, Steve, Paul, Joe, and Zoe Mae: Let's toast to this beautiful feast, to having each other, and..." she paused to look at each one, at the blue eyes of her sons and the green eyes of her daughter, her mother's hazel eyes, and in all of them (even her mother's, with their not-so-hidden condemnation) she saw Vernon, the man she had lived with and loved for fourteen years until he vanished one very green morning in June, already four years ago. She surprised herself by adding, "Let's drink to your father, too, wherever he is." She was light-headed from exhaustion, she thought.

All the children exchanged glances, clinking glasses, raising eyebrows at their mother (for she rarely mentioned him). Eleanor deliberately refused the toast by banging her glass on the tabletop; the amber liquid tossed but didn't spill. The children noticed but said nothing, and Kay was grateful.

"Any more Champagne?" Paul asked.

"None for you," Kay said, pouring herself a little more. "Dean? Steve?"

Steve didn't want any, Dean did. "Dig in, my lovelies," Kay said, and the eating began. She helped herself to the passing platters and watched her good white china plate fill with the colors of fall: scarlet from the cranberries, orange from the yams, yellow squash, deep brown gravy, green string beans, and the pink paleness of turkey.

"You can have mine," Joe said to Paul, sliding his jelly-jar glass across to his twin. There was only a thimbleful of alcohol for the young ones; Zoe Mae hadn't touched hers. (She was sitting on two Plattsburgh phone books, the York County Yellow Pages, and a dictionary, and was still precariously poised over her plate.)

"Hey, Zoe, watch out for the sauce. You almost dipped your elbow in it."

"Dean, hand me that slice of bread, will you?"

"Say please," said Kay.

"Please. I meant to say please."

The snow fell thick and fast, portent of an early and long winter this year. Kay had always loved the snow, even though it buried her car, burdened the porch steps, and generally complicated their lives. It was so clean and soft and magical when it fell, a slow, silent sifting of feathers from a white sky. In a good snowfall all straight edges turned to gentle mounds, their blunt definitions lost: a peeling picnic bench became a plush down coverlet, a heap of trash now a pyramid in mother-of-pearl. She couldn't see anything outside, not even the Short Bay Road, which was only thirty yards from the house. Snow claimed both presence and absence—the familiar world erased, replaced by a clean, unsullied surface. A slate upon which to begin anew (at least for a few hours, until the plows came). Snow tumbled down lightly, not making a sound, already cresting a drift at the bottom of the window. Her mother hated the snow. She and Kay rarely agreed on anything. But still, Eleanor was her mother

(her father had died long ago), and if they could stay away from controversial topics like Vernon, Kay liked having Eleanor beside her, the baby powder scent of her mother's skin within arm's reach.

"Dean, you going to Cathy's later?" Steve asked.

"I guess not. I'll stay here with you guys."

Kay expelled the breath she'd been holding, pleased, hoping no one noticed.

"Now, who's this Cathy person anyway? Reiser?" Eleanor asked. "Didn't her family used to live on the lakeshore?"

"Yes, Grandma. That's her. But now she lives in town. Can you pass the gravy?"

Funny how her mother's hair was still dark and handsome while her own was a crinkly steel-wool gray. Actually it was white, all white. Kay thought she looked older than her mother, who was a trim sixty-four, and who continued to work part-time as a secretary for the York County Court in New Troy. Eleanor had been a widow for twenty-eight years, and after Bill Camden died, she determined to live alone. "That man was the love of my life; I don't want another. I'm saving myself for when we meet again Upstairs." Kay marveled at her mother's faith, which had kept her well and sane for a lifetime. Kay couldn't share it and had nothing with which to replace it, though at times she wished she had.

"Well, if your Grandpa Bill could be here today, this would be a perfect Thanksgiving. The food's delicious," Eleanor said, removing a glob of yam from Zoe Mae's cheek with a napkin. The others echoed their grandmother's praise.

"Is he with Vernon?" Zoe Mae asked. (All the children referred to their father by his first name after he left.)

Eleanor cleared her throat and avoided looking at Kay, who was watching her closely, wondering what kind of explanation would surface. "No, honey, not as far as I know, anyway."

Kay smiled at her mother, thinking that she could be gracious when she wanted to. For once, Zoe Mae didn't pursue the question. Silverware clinked against china, bowls knocked against one another, the gravy boats emptied and Eleanor refilled them, the bread disappeared, the butter diminished, and the green beans remained. Her children were slow eaters, though, like their father. Kay had had to learn to slow down when she married Vernon; otherwise she would finish a meal before her husband had barely begun, for he would stop thoughtfully to adjust his glasses and survey the food, even if it was as simple as eggs and potatoes. Vernon. She picked up her fork and began to eat, responding to requests to pass this or that but remaining uncharacteristically silent, listening instead to the cadences of her children's voices: Dean's already deep and adultlike, Steve's still uneven and unsure of itself, the twins' squeaky and high, barely distinguishable one from the other (although Paul's was one note squeakier), and Zoe Mae's like a chirping sparrow above the rest. Eleanor kept saying, "Yes, and then what happened?" as Zoe Mae told her tale after tale, inventing long-winded adventures about herself and her imaginary twin, Ramona. Only Eleanor had patience enough to follow. Dean was talking to Steve in a deliberately low voice, muffled, Kay concluded, to prevent his mother or grandmother from hearing their conversation. Girls, it must be about girls, Kay thought—that Cathy Reiser whose father ran the saloon in town. Dean, her beautiful, oldest boy. (Look at him brushing his hair behind his ear like Vernon used to, the hair always too short to stay so it fell forward over his eyes, especially when he was eating, and he would patiently push it back again. No matter how often she offered to trim his thick, dark hair, or had trimmed Vernon's thick, sandy hair, that section by the right temple always created a problem.) What was he saying? Could he be in love? It seemed impossible, too soon. Yet, perhaps it was so. He was seventeen, after all, old enough to think he was in love, anyway. As a girl of nine or ten, Kay had already begun to experience mad crushes. But boys were something else. She couldn't know what went on in Dean's head, much less in his heart. Certainly if she knew more about men, she would know what to do about Vernon; she would understand why he'd done what he'd done, and she would have a plan, instead of existing the way she had the last few years in utter confusion, simply refusing to address the whole issue. She kept herself busy with work at the supermarket, in the garden, at canning and preserving, sewing and mending; she found hundreds of tasks to keep Vernon at bay. Initially, when people asked what had happened, she told them Vernon had left without saying why. The simple truth shut them up, and no one asked anymore, although sometimes the children came home hot-cheeked and crying from being taunted by children who repeated stories their parents told, fantasy fabricated by York Ferry gossips with nothing to do. The stories, total speculation, all of them, always involved another woman, complicated by the proclamation that Vernon had never been the same since the war. Kay hated the scandalmongers in town, both men and women, who took on the job of charting the lives of York Ferry's thousand or so inhabitants.

Kay caught Dean's eye, and he smiled broadly, breaking her reverie with a loud, "Hey Mom, why are you so quiet today?"

"Don't say hey to your mother," said Eleanor.

"Why not?" asked Zoe Mae.

"I just feel kind of quiet today, son. Nothing's wrong."

"I didn't say anything was wrong." Dean frowned.

"No, I guess you didn't. But you looked so busy telling secrets down there, I didn't think you'd notice me."

Coloring slightly, Dean mumbled, "I wasn't telling any secrets."

"Then why are you turning all red?" asked Zoe Mae.

"I'm *not* turning red," Dean retorted, blushing, and scraped his chair hard on the linoleum as he rose to carry his plate to the sink.

"Slow down, Dean! Not everyone's finished." Kay was disturbed that he was taking their banter so seriously. "Sit down, please. With your plate. I don't want us to rush. We only have Thanksgiving once a year, you know."

Glowering, he returned to the table and sat. After a moment, he picked up his fork and examined the turkey still left on his plate.

Kay tried to find her way to the dreaminess she'd felt earlier but couldn't get back in. Now the twins were arguing over who should hold the larger end of the wishbone, and then Steve jumped to his feet, hand over mouth, and dashed for the bathroom.

"All right, everyone. Let's take a break before dessert. Plates to the sink, glasses to the counter. Boys, if you can't decide that fairly, I'm going to take it away from both of you."

The children rapidly cleared their places and left the kitchen. Eleanor lit a cigarette, frowning at her daughter. "They do grow fast, don't they?" she said, as if it were Kay's fault.

Nodding sullenly, Kay helped herself to her mother's cigarettes and then got up to make coffee, glancing out the window to reassure herself with the snow. But the snow had stopped, and now she could see the road, the wrecked, rusted tractor across the way; the whole sky was clearing, which upset rather than pleased her. "Damn," she whispered.

"Kayleen, I'm worried about those twins."

"Why?"

"Well, the older boys seem okay, and Zoe Mae doesn't even know there's something missing in this family, but those twins do. Paul especially. And Joe's awfully quiet too—too quiet, if you ask me."

I didn't ask you, Kay thought.

"You need a man around here, Kay. At least when your father died, I only had you to think about, and you weren't a child anymore."

"I had a man around here, Mom, and he'll be back. If not sooner, then later."

"Oh, do you really think so?" her mother asked tartly.

"Mother, today's my favorite day of the year, and I'd really appreciate if you didn't spoil it by insisting on having this conversation."

"What about Mr. Forster at the supermarket? He's a widower, isn't he?"

"Yeah. You interested?" Kay kept her back to her mother as she adjusted the gas under the percolator, sliced the pies, and arranged a tray of cookies.

"Not for me, Kay. For you."

"I'm not interested, Mother. Besides, he's about twenty years older than me."

"Maybe that's better than younger," said Eleanor, implying that Vernon's three-year age difference had something to do with his character.

"His age isn't the point. I'm not interested."

"Well, suit yourself. But I hear he likes you."

"Who'd you hear that from?"

"Bonnie Green, at the bank."

"Well, I don't think Bonnie Green is the authority on Averill Forster's love life."

"She's got the goods on everyone in this town," Eleanor said, "and she's usually more accurate than the *Herald*."

"Fine. Believe what you want. I'm going to see if Steve's all right. Can you watch this coffee for me?" Without waiting for an answer, Kay leaned into the swinging yellow door to the living room. Dean and the twins had built up the fire so that the hearth blazed heat, which might have been nice but now seemed peculiar next to the clearing over the fields where the sun was getting ready to make an appearance. "Steve in the bathroom?"

"Bedroom, I think," Dean said. "Unless he's still puking."

Kay found him huddled over the toilet, Zoe Mae standing beside him with her freckle-spattered hand on his shoulder, trying to peer over him into the bowl.

"Zoe Mae, go ask Grandma for a glass of 7-Up for Steve. Go on!" She pushed her daughter out the door; Zoe Mae was fascinated by anything disgusting. Slugs were her favorite insects.

"Did you throw up your whole dinner?" She stroked Steve's forehead, checking for fever. "Oooh, you're hot. Maybe you've got a bug. It couldn't be the food; the rest of us are fine." Kay paused, wondering if she felt nauseous. No she was just very full. "Are you done, Cookie?"

"I think so." Steve's words were hollowed by the porcelain.

Kay flushed the toilet and then wiped his face with a damp washcloth. He definitely looked sick, his bony shoulders poking out with more severity than usual from his shirt. "Did you eat anything else today that I don't know about?"

Leaning against the white tiled wall, his long legs doubled up like trick rubber pencils, he shook his head, staring fixedly at the floor.

"Well, what then?"

"I smoked a pack of Pall Malls."

"You did what?"

"I took a pack from your carton and went out behind the shed and smoked all of them while you were cooking this morning." Confessing seemed to make him feel better; color slowly returned to his cheeks.

"Oh, Steven. No wonder you're ill. I don't even smoke a whole pack at one sitting." She cupped his chin in her hand and made him look up at her. "I'm not mad at you, Steve. I know everyone has to try them, but I hope you learned something."

He nodded vehemently. "They're gross! I'll never smoke again." Steve was fourteen years old, with the light hair and slight build of his father. Her shy boy, the one she knew least.

"I just wish you hadn't chosen today for the big experiment. Can you sit with us for dessert? Or do you want to lie down?"

"I'm not sure if I need to throw up some more."

"Okay. Sit down with us, and if you don't feel good, just leave the table." It wouldn't be right if one of them were missing, Kay thought.

Zoe Mae returned with half a glass of soda, which Steve drank in one gulp. "Did you try this?"

Zoe Mae nodded. "I love 7-Up."

"Thanks for leaving me some." With that, Steve slid up the wall to his feet, and they all returned to the kitchen.

The sun melted all the snow before dusk, which further disappointed Kay. She didn't go with the rest on their walk but stayed instead at the table, smoking, picking at apple pie crumbs but no longer caring to eat, exhausted now by the whole Thanksgiving ordeal. There were mountains of dirty dishes, pots, pans, and the oven needed a thorough cleaning. Eleanor was with the children, and Kay wished that Vernon were at the table with her, sharing their after-dinner cigarette and coffee. This was his seat, where she was sitting, where she had sat since the first anniversary of his disappearance when she realized he wasn't coming home any time soon. After surviving fourteen years of marriage, Kay had figured they could survive most anything. She'd finally had a daughter, and although she would have tried for another, Vernon said five was enough. Who could have predicted his behavior—quiet, sensible Vernon, the most reliable mechanic in the North Country? She'd received two letters from him over four years, two letters she hadn't told anyone about, both of them containing money, asking forgiveness, asking that she write. But she couldn't forgive, and she didn't write. It was the only power she had over him, this ability to withhold communication.

The phone rang.

Who would call on Thanksgiving? Everyone was at home with family. Except Vernon. Could it be him, calling from Alaska? She didn't move, and the phone rang and rang. When it didn't stop after ten rings, she felt positive it was him, could sense his presence in the room, looked down to see his arms gripping the armrest, the suntanned hair on his fingers, the fingernails that stayed black no matter how hard he scrubbed, his wedding band snug, just over the knuckle. Her wedding band, which she was twirling with her thumb. Her arm was on the armrest now, her hand gripping the wood so tightly her skin drained of color as the phone rang and rang, Vernon on the other end at the other end of the country or the world, and only he could know that they might be returning from the lake at around this time, so he would let it ring and ring, hoping they might walk in at any moment. What would she say to him? What would he say? Would it stop ringing the minute she got up to answer?

The telephone was a heavy old black model which sat beside the toaster. Kay could see it from where she sat in front of the big window, Vernon's favorite spot. She'd never heard the house so quiet, or the ring so loud, or urgent. It must have rung fifty times by now, and still it kept on. As she stubbed out her cigarette, she noticed her hands were shaking, shaking uncontrollably, and her stomach lurched and heaved. She couldn't move. She wanted to yell into the phone, "You bastard! How could you leave us like this?" She wanted to hear him say, "I've had enough. You win, Kay; I'm coming home." She wanted to say, "I miss you, Vernon," for she missed him unbearably. She lit another cigarette, scarcely able to make the flame of the match connect with the tobacco, and still the phone rang. She couldn't stand it, picturing Vernon in some frozen phone booth, his glasses fogged, his hands ungloved and stiff with cold. She moved the chair back slowly, afraid that any sudden movement would stop the ringing. It was hard to stand. Her legs trembled so that she had to keep a hand on the tablecloth to steady herself as she made her way across the room. It might not be Vernon after all, she told herself. It could be a wrong number, or one of her relatives, or a friend of the children—anyone at all.

It took forever to walk across the kitchen, which was not an especially large room. She was scared to move any faster, afraid to rupture the unreal stillness of the house. It seemed as if the phone had always been ringing, and she had always been moving in slow motion, trying to reach it. She was approaching, her arm wavering but stretching to grasp the receiver when the door burst open and everyone piled in, and Dean was running pell-mell toward the phone, shouting, "I've got it! I've got it! It's Cathy!" and both Dean and Kay were reaching for the phone when it stopped ringing.

"Oh well. She'll call back. I know she will." Dean smiled at his mother, a wide exuberant smile, and Kay knew that her son really was in love.

Gold Dust Hotel
Whitehorse
Yukon Territory
Dec. 23

Dear Kay,

It's getting to be a habit now, isn't it—me writing you at
Christmas and sending money, as if I were some rich faraway
uncle. Still, you haven't written, but I keep hoping. I'm not
giving up on you yet. You'll find $800 in this money order. I
want you to buy something big for yourself, and with the rest
some surprises for the kids—bikes or something. I do remember their birthdays, you know, even though I bet you
think I've forgotten. I considered sending cards, but maybe
it's better for them not to be reminded of me too much. Do
you show them these letters? You probably should—Dean's
an adult now. He'd want to know. Do you tell them where I
am? I go back and forth on the narrow gauge between
Skagway and Whitehorse. I'm the chief mechanic up here—
mostly the only one too. How's that Le Sabre running? I bet
it's got a lot of miles on it by now. You could replace it with
something used but decent—have Dean check the car out for
you first. I was training him to be a good engine man. Does
he work at the garage with Henry now?

You must be wondering why I'm not back in Europe when I
keep saying I'm leaving for there. It's hard to explain why I
get cold feet whenever I set a date. I've got this picture in my
head, you see, of Antwerp in the winter of 1944; the cars, the
clothes, the signs on the restaurants, the GIs and Brits clog-
ging the streets. Everything's stuck in my head at this frozen
moment when I saw Irene, sweeping the sidewalk in front of
what used to be her parents' grocery store. Somebody else
was running it, but she still swept the pavement every morning like she used to before the war. I asked her directions for
the post office, in English of course, and she answers me in
English. In fact, she's so excited to practice her English that
she walks me there, and then I invite her for a coffee. She
had short black hair and porcelain skin, though she was awfully thin, and she wore some horribly drab clothing—a cast-
off and oversize school uniform from a nearby convent. Gray
and blue, I think it was, designed for somebody twice her
weight. I was a green 21, with all of my hair back then, standing straight up to God with a crewcut, feeling righteous and

28

proud in my Air Force mechanic's coveralls. Thought I'd been through a lot already for a kid from Lake Champlain, a brassy country boy strutting like a rooster around Antwerp because I knew in my gut that we were going to whip those Germans. Then I met her. I wanted to protect her. How can you protect someone from a bomb? I knew when I left her, somehow, that she wouldn't be there when I returned. I felt responsible, do you see? And I failed her. It's my New Year's resolution to go back and explain this to Irene, assuming she has a grave.

Kay, please send news of yourself and the kids. I'm trying hard to be honest with you. I know I could call, but I'm afraid you'll hang up on me. I know this is hard. The guy at the Vet Center in Fairbanks told me that 20% of the men who came in on the Normandy beaches went home with shell shock, although I bet that number's way too low. I don't think *I* have shell shock though—I have something else.

Vernon

Chapter 3

1965

Eleanor's porch nearly disappeared under the vines and huge heart-shaped leaves that intertwined the full length and breadth of her small house's western front. She no longer took her late-night tea there for the darkness frightened her, breathing heavily through the thick stems and fronds. But when there was light, the porch became a yellow terrarium, and inside it one felt like a shooting fern, a sprout on the forest floor finding comfort and succor from the sun. It was a fine place for the grandchildren when the strong summer rays steeped the green enough to illuminate the floor with gold; there they would play War for hours, protected from the intense heat, cards flipping steadily. Through the afternoons and early evenings, a dull glow forced the objects and bodies on the porch to bear some kind of halo, difficult to decipher but tangible enough to those who believed.

"Why do I have to go to church, Grandma? I never go with Mom and the boys." Zoe Mae, eight years old, chafed against the stiff starched dress her grandmother had forced her into after a breakfast of pancakes, bacon and eggs. The lace collar scraped her earlobes.

"Because your mother has failed to look out for your spiritual growth, Zoe Mae, I've vowed to undertake that task. From now on, you'll stay with me Saturday nights so we can walk ourselves to church in the mornings." Eleanor sniffed the loamy smell of

June sifting through the vines. "I'm not so concerned about the boys missing out; a girl needs God more than men. There's a hard road ahead, sweet child, studded with nasty nails and tiresome obstacles the Lord may have sent your way for a road test. If you're not prepared, the highway itself will defeat you, pierce the air right out of your tires or spit hot oil when your earthly engine fails. You can't be barefoot, Zoe Mae, and you better not be caught naked. Church is like a spiritual department store which outfits you for life. You have to go back regularly to keep maintained."

Grandmother and granddaughter sat in the rickety wicker settee before starting their walk to the North Country Presbyterian Church, which was only three doors down from Eleanor's house on the southern end of York Ferry. Occasionally the sheriff hid in its parking lot to trap strangers ignoring the in-town speed limit. Eleanor told him she thought it sacrilegious to use God's buildings for speed traps, but Sheriff Green just laughed. "You've got to change with the times, Mrs. Camden," he said.

The times did not please Eleanor. She had defaulted in her mission to teach her daughter to revere God; she hoped for redemption and a second chance with Zoe Mae.

"If I'm getting new clothes at church, then why do I have to wear this?" Zoe Mae asked, pulling the elastic cuffs away from her skin, hugging herself in a great pout.

The dress was a veritable heirloom, an official Sunday gown passed down through the generations, hemmed and taken in or out to suit its various wearers. As a child, Kay had seemed a pious beauty in that dress, Eleanor remembered, yet her daughter, too, had rebelled against its confines. When Eleanor had worn it, she adored the smell and finery of a dress with such singular purpose: the worship of God. While Zoe Mae looked pretty in all of its lace, her red hair and green eyes a lively contrast to the austere white, she moved as if her skin were crawling with ants. The way she eyed the apple tree out front gave Eleanor visions of revolt, of the short legs clambering up the trunk, scraping shins and ripping tights and linen against the gnarled, venerable limbs.

"You'll get used to it. You'll be all uncomfortable in church at first, because you'll think the minister's talking in general and doesn't have anything important to say, but one Sunday you'll sit up so straight in all that reverent lace because you'll discover he's talking to *you*." Eleanor pressed her forefinger on the tip of Zoe Mae's nose. "And on that day you'll be comfortable with both the dress and God."

They marched out together, hand in hand, Eleanor in her suit of robin's egg blue with matching shoes and a newly dyed bonnet. On the sidewalk they fell in with Henry Leicester and his wife, June, walking briskly. Henry grunted hello, awkward in his old suit, his bulky body bursting from cuffs and hems, pant legs too short, arms too tight. The auto mechanic's knuckles showed scrapes and bruises, his fingernails black. Henry had taken over the York Ferry Garage from Eleanor's son-in-law, who was, by all accounts, the better mechanic. In the five years since Vernon had disappeared, the garage had failed, slowly but surely. June, in her smart yellow dress which called attention to her cigarette-pallor skin, nodded approvingly at Zoe Mae, a tobacco-stained finger reaching out to touch the girl's cascade of brilliant curls.

"I see you've decided to educate at least one of those grandchildren, Mrs. Camden," she said.

Eleanor grabbed Zoe Mae away from the woman's touch and stepped off the sidewalk, pretending to adjust the girl's barrettes. "You two go on. We'll meet up with you later, I'm sure."

It was one thing for Eleanor to criticize Kay and the way she brought up her five children, but it was quite another for June Leicester, of all people, to do the same. It was a known fact of local lore that when June was still a Morissey, she had participated in the carnal pleasures with more than one otherwise married man. God had punished June by denying her children of her own, and so she had declared herself an authority on the ways of all mothers.

"I don't like her," Zoe Mae whispered as they resumed their pace, flanked by other families with whom Eleanor exchanged good mornings. "She looks like a rhinoceros."

"Shush. Don't repeat that, please," Eleanor whispered, though inside she was laughing, because June did have a great honker of a nose, and Eleanor had spent long hours trying to describe exactly what that profile called to mind. "We learn in church to be Christian and kind to our neighbors, Zoe Mae, not petty and small."

Once seated, Zoe Mae was bored immediately, the tips of her sneakers barely grazing the floor. Eleanor had duly consented to the sneakers upon concluding that the girl's white patent leather shoes would no longer fit her plump feet. The antique dress and red plaid Keds made an odd match, which served, however temporarily, to attract attention to Zoe Mae.

Minister Eldridge greeted them, congratulated a couple in Whalen, a tiny mountain hamlet, for the birth of their first child, and lamented the death of a teenager from York Ferry who had perished in a car accident the night before, apparently the result of a drag race and alcohol; the victim's car was filled with empty beer bottles that had broken in the crash and slashed the boy's body to shreds. A wave of murmurs swept the congregation as the news and commentary flowed among the churchgoers, eddying against the rear pews, then surging out again into the crowd. Eleanor's elderly neighbor shook her head, thin lips pursed. "I knew that boy would come to trouble," she said. "I used to see him stealing pop from the IGA." The woman shook her head slowly. "I told his mother, but she didn't care. Can you imagine?"

Eleanor also shook her head, thinking of her grandsons growing up fatherless in an unpredictable world. As the minister went on about the untimely passing of a young life, her memory unreeled the funeral of her husband twenty-nine years ago this December, a life still decidedly within the boundaries of youth.

Forty years old, dead of a massive coronary, snatched by God for a reason or purpose it had taken Eleanor these three decades to fully comprehend. Her son-in-law's desertion clarified everything: Bill Camden had been called early on so that Eleanor would be free and able to attend to the glaring needs of her grandchildren later, when she might have been nursing a sick husband through old age. She herself had the constitution of a workhorse, but her husband had suffered all ailments to which the flesh is heir: colds, flu, asthma, nerves. And poor Bill had a weak heart as well.

Although it required reining in her natural will, Eleanor stopped short at putting herself in the role of Vernon's surrogate. She didn't, after all, live with her daughter and grandchildren, nor did she support them financially. Yet, she knew Kay looked to her for help in making big decisions (encouraging Dean, for example, to quit the York Ferry Garage when it was clear he could no longer bear to work there) even when Kay disagreed and sometimes disregarded her mother's opinion. For this Eleanor had remained a widow. She kept her figure up, prided herself on looking neat and respectable. She appeared younger than her age, and older men still eyed her with interest. At her job at the assessor's office, men from all over York County arrived in need of her assistance with the Byzantine bureaucracy of tax. She'd worked there nearly thirty-five years and knew the arcane details inside and out. Her boss, a young college graduate, hoped she would put off retirement for as long as possible.

Now the minister was talking about the perils of excessive drink, of the sins of the flesh. Eleanor couldn't help but think of Mr. Donald O'Donnell, her previous boss, whom God had tempted her with all through the 1950s, a lovely, gentle man who had waited and waited for her to come to him, to put aside her objections to his married state, and to acknowledge their mutual attraction. He never pressed; they never spoke of it, but for eleven years they sensed one another's hunger, leaning over forms together, his hands just an inch from hers on the green desk blotter, his cologne sweet, nearly intoxicating, the two of them alone in the office after hours at tax time, their faces so close they might have kissed without moving more than their lips. Oh, it had been a trial, and she'd nearly succumbed, but when she'd asked God for help, her will returned. She resisted, saving herself for the real work ahead of scouting the road for the fatherless children: pushing aside the stones and spikes, posting bright warning signs on every pothole. Mr. O'Donnell had stayed true to his wife; she thought of him often.

Suddenly noticing the hymnal in her neighbor's hand, Eleanor leafed through her own black book, pretending to read along while she tried, unsuccessfully, to make out the page number. She had strayed from the sermon, providing a poor example for her granddaughter.

But Zoe Mae was listening now to the minister's words, her back perfectly straight, mouth open.

"Jesus had no earthly father but a heavenly one," Minister Eldridge was saying. "The ways in which we understand our Father's wisdom are multifold and rich."

Eleanor felt Zoe Mae's small hand pulling at her sleeve. She leaned over to hear her granddaughter whisper, "I don't have an earthly father either. But I have a mother."

The sun entered the church through its small stained glass windows, rose and green filtering light beneath the high ceiling. Dust danced in the confetti-colored rays, spinning the whirling particles, and Zoe Mae, no longer paying attention to the minister, sat utterly transfixed, her toes no longer trying to reach the floor, her hands limp on the hard wood pew, neck craned.

Eleanor whispered that she would explain all of this later, after church, and without Zoe Mae noticing, she took her granddaughter's fingers into her lap, enlacing them with her own, and prayed for guidance.

Skagway, Alaska
May 31
Depot Hotel

Dear Kay,

Am I a coward? Is that how you thought of me during our 14
years together? Since I last wrote, I made three different
plane reservations and cancelled every one of them, twice be-
forehand and once when I was packed, holding my suitcase,
having gotten as far as the lobby. During the same period of
time I nearly quit my job and bought a ticket home, though I
didn't do that either. Still no word from you, but if these letters aren't being returned to me, then I suppose you're re-
ceiving them. Did you get the money order I sent at
Christmas? I'm sorry there was no note; I just couldn't write
anything then.

Finally it's spring here, almost six years since I left York Ferry.
Funny how we call the Lake Champlain area the North
Country, because it's not really north at all compared to here.
The day I left is very clear in my mind: the smell of the earth
I'd turned for your gardens the evening before, the way the
farmhouse shrunk in the pickup's rear-view mirror as I drove
off to the train station. The way your hair blended into the
pillowcase that morning. I remember it clearly but it seems
like another me entirely who lived those years and followed
through on the day of departure. The soldier who fell in love
with a girl in Antwerp is someone else too. I'm all in pieces.
Fragments of me have splintered off like bits of shrapnel all
over the damn world. Dean will be 20 next year, the same age
as Irene. She was like no one I'd ever met—frail and fragile
on the outside, with a small, quiet voice, but she wasn't frail at
all, not inside. You're the opposite of that, I think. I can't say
why I fell in love with her—is there ever a rational reason?
something you could point a fingernail to and say there! *this*
is it. This is why. I remember the way she would translate
something for me, standing on tiptoe, whispering at my neck
so that I could feel her breath there. Do you understand
now? she would say. Do you understand now? And when I
said yes, I understood, she would smile at me as if I'd given
her some great gift. Or perhaps she was simply pleased with
herself for translating, but she'd smile away as if there was no

tomorrow. And there was no tomorrow. We spent one night together, she and I, just one night. It was very daring of her. She told her old father, who she'd hidden with during the war, taking care of him when he lost the use of his eyes from diabetes. She even introduced me to him, but he didn't speak any English. It was just a lot of nodding. Still, he was her father and he couldn't protect her anymore. I guess she protected him during those years in the room with no windows. I told him I would take care of Irene. I promised.

When I found out she was dead, I figured he was dead too. All of my buddies were out drinking and carousing because we'd beaten the Germans at Bastogne against tough odds, and I was falling apart. I don't even remember how I ended up getting run over crossing the damn street. Two broken legs to end the war with—what a hero I was—honorable discharge and all. Shipped back to Plattsburgh to heal, and then I met you. I was so grateful when you seemed to like me, Kay. Was it wrong for us to marry? I didn't ever lie to you, and although I didn't tell you about Irene, I felt you'd understand. Do you? Do you understand now?

Vernon

Chapter Four

1967

Along the Lakeshore Drive, from its southern end near Old Church Road to its northern tip at Elbow Peninsula Beach, Steve ran. Before the sun rose in summer, and late on winter afternoons, his long legs gracefully carried him beside the water and then up Quarry Hill to Route 22 before he circled back to the lake. He wore gray sweatpants and a matching T-shirt, both imprinted with the SUNY-Plattsburgh logo, "Conquer Through the Mind." His mother had presented them to him last week on his seventeenth birthday, knowing how fiercely he wanted the scholarship. It was mid-January, and Steve watched the trailing vapors of his breath nearly freeze in the biting air. His size-12 feet hit the pavement with a steady, comforting rhythm, the sound of his sneakers on cement a mesmerizing accompaniment to conscious thought, which he tried to narrow down to nothing, to concentrate only on stretching one leg forward after the other. He was working on elongating his stride now, and his loping arms swung like a pendulum, like two pendulums, as he passed the vast houses of stone and deep red brick, every one of them shuttered and dead for nine months of the year. They looked like furious faces, Steve thought, angry at being left so long alone. There was no sun today, no wind, only the numbing cold of the North Country winter. Earlier, during his warm-up, Steve heard the radio forecaster announce the temperature at

15 degrees, and falling.

Fortunately, no ice lingered on the road to trip him up. The winter had been strangely snowless so far, maple branches looming like black skeletons against the sky, ravens cawing and traveling in groups, as if afraid. When snow or hoarfrost laced the tree limbs, this stretch of the lakeshore was to Steve the most magical in all of York Ferry, like an illustration from a child's story book. When you could see the lake endlessly white between the mansions, when the houses seemed, with their feathered lintels and sloping gabled roofs, to be sleepily pleased with themselves, they looked like children who'd been caught napping without having been asked.

Steve passed a three-story stone colossus with two chimneys, a swimming dock, and a motorboat port in back. He'd been inside the house, and some of the others, too, when he did odd jobs during the summer season: mowing lawns, fixing docks damaged during the winter, hauling garbage to the dump. The things these people threw away: entire living room sets, perfectly good, they replaced with newer, more fashionable ones. He'd thought his mother would have gladly gotten rid of the Pinnys' worn corduroy couches for the Richardsons' barely used ones, but Kay refused even to see them. On principle, he supposed.

"Let someone else have them," she'd said. "Bring them up by the Smithfields. They've probably never even had a couch."

"I can't drive this heavy truck up that dirt road, Mom. Be realistic." Steve thought his mother was being illogical. The Smithfields, hill people who rarely came to town, lived a half-hour up a rutted fire road no longer maintained by the county. No one knew exactly how many Smithfields there were in the sprawling trailer-shanty compound. Steve had prevailed on that point.

"Well, just dump them, then. That's what they pay you for," his mother ordered.

Steve ran closer to the shoulder when he heard a vehicle approach from behind. The road was rarely traveled in winter, when most people stayed on Route 22 to get from here to there. In summer, of course, the Lakeshore Drive was heavily used. A few times each season the summer people imported traffic jams to York Ferry. When one family had a party and invited all the others, plus their friends and friends of friends from the city, they would hire a handful of local boys to park the cars. Up and down both sides of the Drive, gleaming Cadillacs and Chryslers in colors so bright they hurt the eye lined the wide avenue. The boys wore sunglasses and acted tough, throwing their shoulders back as if they always drove cars smelling of leather and cologne.

Now the road was bare, empty but for the truck behind him, which refused to pass. Finally he turned around, still running, to discover three York Ferry girls in a battered Ford pickup, first waving furiously at him then planting kisses on their clouded windows before honking and speeding away, yelling something he couldn't understand. At first, he felt flattered, believing their gestures to be some form of girls' appreciation, an area about which Steve knew little. He had always been overpowered by his older brother's reputation and good looks. Although Dean was already married, his status as the best catch in his class still haunted his younger brother and would probably linger to daunt the twins.

Without breaking stride, watching the pickup fade in the darkness, he continued on, the euphoria of the first five miles now disintegrating into fatigue, spawning a gnawing despair that he would never be strong enough or fast enough to make the Plattsburgh trials. After further reflection on the girls' visitation, he concluded that they had been mocking him with their exaggerated kisses. He hadn't been able to see their faces clearly, but he could guess who they were: Louise, Ceil, Margaret, the brassy group in his class who were always drinking and carousing, racing the boys on the two-lane death-mile over by the Champlain Bar & Grill. He was glad he had only a year left of high school, one more year of seeing the same monotonous York County faces every morning and afternoon, grade after grade. At SUNY, there would be people from all over New York State and from other parts of the country as well, even foreigners.

Squinting to read his watch, Steve ordered himself to run the hill once more before heading home. The heat his muscles had generated diminished as the cold grew more bitter.

Quarry Hill loomed before him, an average incline grown to monstrous proportion. He fought the urge to walk, jogging slowly past the graveyard. He passed a handful of sagging wooden houses, their chimneys smoking a sooty silhouette against the gray. There was a lone trailer at the summit, home to a family of ten, which included four generations. Stumbling with fatigue, he gratefully turned onto Route 22 for the half-mile south to the turn-off at the Short Bay Road, from where he would sprint to the farmhouse. A pair of headlights flashed by, then another, and another. People were driving home to Port Elizabeth and the smaller villages from their jobs in New Troy, county seat, the largest town south of Plattsburgh to which York Ferry people might commute. Route 22 linked all the villages along the lake and the interior, connecting the small places no interstate would be interested in; York Ferry itself would be inaccessible to the Adirondack Northway, which was already under construction, two miles west. Route 22 dipped and turned a good thirty miles south to Marysville at the southern tip of the county, which would have access to the highway because of its bridge connecting New York and Vermont over Lake Champlain. There were no other bridges for sixty miles north—the next one was nearly in Canada—only the seasonal ferries to transport tourists across the watery state borders.

The Pinny farmhouse was the sole dwelling in Madnan's Valley, although the Bakers, whom no one had ever met, owned most of the land. Steve sprinted toward the bright porch lights, welcoming him home. His ten-year-old sister was sitting in front of the woodstove playing cards, her own version of double-solitaire War. Zoe Mae looked up when he entered, flashed her dazzling grin, exposing very pink gums that framed a red hot jawbreaker, and announced, "Pee-Yoo! You stink!"

Laughing, he charged toward her. "Zoe Mae, I can't stand all the compliments you always dish out." He tickled her belly, making her roll in contortions on the floor, shrieking with pleasure and irritation, her card game destroyed.

Voices and the sound of clattering plates, silverware scraping china, crept through the closed kitchen door, and the smell of cigarettes hung heavily, infuriating Steve because no one respected his desire to keep his lungs in respectable condition. The twins smoked. They were only twelve, but already Steve had seen them hiding their Lucky Strikes. Dean and Cathy smoked, his mother smoked. He lived and breathed in a cluster of smokestacks, all conspiring to ruin his chances at the trials; only his room was safe.

"Zoe Mae?" He stopped tickling, and she panted loudly, as if she'd run the seven miles alongside him. "Listen, I'll stop for good if you promise me now and forever that you'll never smoke. Deal?" His wriggling fingers wavered in the air over her belly, threatening continuance.

"I promise. I swear I'll never take even one puff of a cigarette my whole entire life, and after death too. Okay? Don't tickle me anymore. I have to get back to my game; I was just ready to win."

"Against who?"

"Ramona."

Steve considered arguing with her about her undying imaginary twin sister. He thought she was getting too old for such devices, but his mother said there was nothing to worry about. She thought Zoe Mae was jealous that the boys had so many brothers, and she didn't get even one sister.

Hoping for a good dinner and a peaceful meal, Steve leaned into the yellow door, bracing himself for the raft of smoke which hit him square in the face, along with the rising voice of his sister-in-law.

"You know, where I grew up we didn't have to settle for the lousy public school." Cathy's angry tone always seemed to Steve to be surprisingly powerful for such a petite woman. "At parochial school I actually learned something."

"How was your run, Steven dear?" asked his mother, obscured behind a Pall Mall cloud. He could tell she was relieved to change the subject. Dean was pacing the room by the big window, as Steve could vaguely remember his father doing, and the twins were washing dishes, or playing at washing them; they'd begun their nightly water fight.

"Cut it out, goddamnit!" Dean snapped, then looked at Kay apologetically. "Sorry, Mom."

"Boys," Kay sighed and lit another cigarette. "Please do that quietly, and then you may leave. See what your sister's up to. Steve, there's a plate of meat loaf and vegetables in the oven for you. Come sit. You must be exhausted."

From the far end of the table, he studied his sister-in-law, who was glaring at Dean for some new reason unknown to Steve. He didn't like her; he didn't understand her at all. She was always hostile, her rather high voice perpetually raised in scorn or indignation. Cathy had shoulder-length blonde hair and deep green eyes, a body boys at school still talked about and girls envied. He found it hard to reconcile her beauty with his dislike. Mostly, she ignored Steve, and he took her dismissal as indicative of his lesser worth when compared to Dean. He ate without attempting to join their conversation; the food was hot but dried out, and he could smell his sweat stinking up the room. Zoe Mae was right.

"Sorry, honey, but we don't live in Con-nec-ti-cut!" The way Dean separated the word into syllables made evident his contempt for her home state. "The York Ferry school system worked fine for me, thank you, and it'll be just fine for our children, too."

Steve wondered if Cathy were pregnant again; she'd miscarried the first time. It was just like her to pick an argument over something years in the future.

"What do you think, Steve?" his brother asked. "You have any problem with our li'l' country school? Cathy thinks it's not good enough for her blood. Although, I should add, she didn't do so bad there. Found me, after all."

Their constant sarcasm made Steve uncomfortable, and he did not want to join in. "Well, if I get the scholarship, I'll say York Ferry was great, and if I don't, then I'll have something to blame it on." He shrugged. "I don't really have anything to compare it to."

"Bingo," said Cathy, pointing her cigarette at him. "That's the whole point."

"You'll get the scholarship if you keep working so hard." His mother smiled at him, trying to deflate Cathy's wrath.

"Yeah, you're going to do fine," Dean said. "Why are you worrying about it so much? The trials aren't until fall, right?"

Steve nodded. "Takes at least a year to get in good shape, though. I don't think I started early enough."

"Well, those drunks who pass for coaches at the high school aren't much help, I'm sure," Cathy snorted.

Kay stood up. "You two stay as long as you like, but I'm tired." She crushed her cigarette into the brimming ashtray Dean had made for her in kindergarten; it was in the shape of a lopsided sunflower head, its bright yellow petals long faded to dull ochre by decades of cigarettes. "I'm going to check Zoe Mae's homework, then to bed. Good night."

"Are we done, Mom?" Paul asked.

Kay surveyed the sink and counter. "Wipe up that puddle by the drainer, and then you can go. Thank you, boys."

They raced to do it, then fled the room just behind their mother. Like the rest of the family, Steve did not want to be alone with Dean and Cathy. He gulped the last of the meat, cleaned his plate with a slice of bread, then hastily ran his dish under the tap. "I gotta shower," he said to the now quiet couple, whose silence indicated a brooding calm before the next crash of thunder. "See you later."

Later, in the room he once shared with Dean, Steve lay sleepless. Cathy and his brother had left in a whirl of slamming doors and bitter words, and after the Jeep revved up and disappeared down the driveway, Kay called from her bedroom to the rest of the family, "Hallelujah!"

Steve wanted to talk to her about the trials but couldn't bring himself to bother her. Cathy's visits always left her depressed. "Of all the girls he had to *have* to marry, I just wish he hadn't gone and slept with her," Kay liked to say after her encounters with her daughter-in-law. "She's just not very nice."

The rock-and-roll station in Plattsburgh came in faintly on his transistor, which he kept close to his ear. The Left Banke was singing, "Just walk away, Renée, you won't see me follow you back home..." which made him again reconsider the girls in the truck. They were making fun of him, he was sure. Steve was tall and gangly, suffering now from an extraordinary inundation of acne and its scars, whose surface area could rival Zoe Mae's freckles. Broad-shouldered and confident Dean, a reasonable six feet tall compared with Steve's excessive six-foot-three, had the clear, never-blemished skin of his mother. He knew how to talk to people, knew particularly how to talk to girls. Dean was more like his mother in all ways, Steve thought, and everyone liked them both. He was like his father—even Kay admitted that some-times—quiet and moody and uncomfortable with strangers. When Steve was in elementary school, he'd acquired the nick-name of "The Deaf Mute" because he spoke so rarely. In third grade, they'd watched a film about Helen Keller, and for weeks afterward, kids would come up to him in the playground and grab his hand, pulling at his fingers, shouting "Wa-ter, wa-ter." Or they'd douse him thoroughly, pushing his head under the spigot. He would run away, out of the schoolyard and down to the lake, where only the gulls and an occasional heron would take note of his presence. He'd run first out of need, later out of pleasure, and now from a vague sense of desperation. Running was the only thing he did well, although he feared he didn't do it well enough. He wanted to be exceptional, to disappear out ahead of all his peers, leaving only a trail of smoke like a hero in a Saturday cartoon.

In October, after a summer spent furiously training along his circular route, Steve drove to Plattsburgh for the trials. Kay had offered to join him, but he preferred to go alone. Bringing his mother along to a university might give others cause to ridicule him. No one else from York Ferry was there, but boys from all over the state, dressed in bright new track shorts and T-shirts, filled the modern gymnasium, its gleaming equipment outshining everything in the York Ferry Amalgamated School District's inventory. He'd decided it would be bad luck to wear his SUNY sweats and so settled on a plain white shirt and navy shorts faded pastel from long use and countless washings. Even before his turn, he felt gloomy about his chances, inadequate beside the others. There were black boys from New York City, a place whose name alone intimidated him, and other dark-skinned faces speaking foreign languages; he identified Spanish but was baffled by other tongues. A handful of boys with curly black hair and olive complexions spoke heavily accented English which Steve found nearly impossible to decipher. He'd never been in such a conglomeration of colors and accents and strangeness. All of them, he imagined, ran faster than he did.

Adrenaline raced in his veins, the room evaporating from vision as Steve ran faster than he'd thought possible, pushing himself beyond previous ability, his footfalls echoing like gunshot. The man with the stopwatch nodded as Steve came in second in the mile run. "Good job, son. Excellent time," he said, writing it down on his clipboard. "You'll hear from us by February. I think we'll have good news. But don't stop running if we can't give you a scholarship this year. It's very competitive this fall. I've never seen it this tough."

Along the Lakeshore Drive, Steve ran and ran. Autumn gave way, in a wind-whipped flurry of brilliant leaves, to a gentler winter, this one full of snow. He dodged the patches of ice, followed the tracks of cars in new powder, managing in spite of all obstacles to lower his average mile time. He paced himself with the passing cars, especially one white station wagon that returned nearly every night to follow the same course. Carol Ann, another senior in his class, would drive alongside blasting her radio, eating peanuts, singing along with the Beatles as the d.j. spun the new tunes from "Sergeant Pepper's Lonely Hearts Club Band." The SUNY coach's words of praise formed the litany which calibrated Steve's running. "Good job, son. Never so tough. Never so tough," as Carol Ann serenaded him in her melodious voice with the words to "Within You, Without You."

In January, Steve learned he hadn't made the final cut. A courteous letter from the office of financial aid informed him they were unable to award him a scholarship based on his running, but there were many other options for financing his education. SUNY Plattsburgh had accepted him to the school. Kay and Dean tried their hardest to persuade Steve to attend, but he refused to consider it. If he couldn't go on his running ability, then he didn't want to go at all. He had no great interest in college; he regretted only that he could never again run on that gleaming indoor track.

Instead of doing odd jobs that summer on the lakeshore, Steve was hired as a maintenance man at the summer camp for rich city kids in Port Elizabeth. The terms included room and board if he wanted them.

"Listen, Mom. I'm going to stay at the camp," he announced to Kay. "It makes more sense than driving back and forth every day."

It was the afternoon after his graduation, which he had not attended. He and Kay were sitting on the porch of the sagging farmhouse, surveying the deep green mountains to the west and the shimmering lake to the east. The day had started hot, threatening a searing summer, yet a vague breeze managed to make its way up from the water and snake around the house, nearly drying the sweat on Steve's brow.

"You're just dying to get out of here, aren't you?" In faded blue jeans and an old workshirt of Vernon's, his mother looked tired. She'd worked in the garden all morning, her crown of braids unraveling, and now she was smoking a cigarette, drinking lemonade, and sounding angry. "When you go, that leaves me and the twins and Zoe Mae here. Three restless kids and one exhausted old lady."

"I'll only be twenty miles up the road, Mom. It's just for two months. And Dean's barely five miles away. You know he'd come in a second if you needed anything." Already he felt guilty for leaving, for even wanting to leave, fearing he was too much like his father who had left for the day and never returned.

"Oh, Steven. It'll be for more than the summer. Once you get a taste for living on your own, you won't want to come back. I guarantee it."

Still aching from his morning run, Steve massaged his calves. Since his defeat at the trials, he had expanded his route to ten miles. Now that there was no pressure for speed, he found himself taking pleasure in the pure act of running. His five-mile euphoria lasted longer and longer. He noticed things he'd never seen before: the red and pink geraniums in windowboxes on the lakeshore mansions; the sinuous curves of Madnan's Ridge, which resembled a naked woman lying on her side, facing him as he ran west up Quarry Hill. He pretended the dark patches of pine forest made up her breasts and crotch, and all the smaller ridges fanning northward were her curling, curving hair. So far, Steve's only experience with girls was between the pages of *Playboy*. As popular and outgoing as Dean had been, Steve was his opposite. Carol Ann had become his only friend, an odd acquaintance. She was obese but very sweet, and people thought they were romantically involved. Steve didn't appreciate being called "Fat Carol Ann's Mute Man," and the variations thereon. But mostly they talked together after his runs about what would happen to them in the future. They called themselves the charter members of the York Ferry Outcast Club. Carol Ann planned to enter secretarial school up in Plattsburgh so that she could use her typing skills; she didn't mention marriage. Steve hadn't been drafted, and though he felt ambivalent about Vietnam, he would have gone to serve his country, as Vernon had. He didn't intend to enlist, however, as several of his classmates had done. Carol Ann faithfully returned each night to drive beside him, leaving a trail of peanut shells and cigarette butts, her singing voice a new accompaniment to his footfalls.

"You'll have one less big mouth to feed, anyway," he said to his mother, hoping to make her laugh, but she frowned instead down at the garden.

"You don't have a big mouth, Steve. And I hope you're not considering my food budget as a factor in your decision. Once there were seven of us, you know, and we managed just fine."

"I'm not, Mom. I didn't mean that." He stood beside her, looking down at her abundant white hair springing from the confining braids; once it had been dark, but after the twins were born, all the color drained out. Kay was of average height, but beside her tallest son, she seemed tiny. She put her arm around his waist and pressed her face against his sweaty chest. He thought she might cry, and he didn't know what to do. Kay was always so cool and practical, even or especially in crises, as when Paul slashed his leg open on the front gate, or when Zoe Mae fell off the roof the night she decided to fly down to the lake with Ramona. He'd never seen his mother weep. In both emergencies, Kay had piled them all into the LeSabre, driven fast but not dangerously to the hospital in Plattsburgh, where Paul was sewn back up with seventeen stitches, and his sister had her broken leg set. His mother always knew what to do and did it without fuss. Steve couldn't bear to see her lose her composure; his departure seemed to him nothing in comparison to what she'd been through already.

"I'll come back after the summer. I swear."

"Oh, I don't want that. I mean, I don't want you to go, but I don't think you should stay here either. Your father…" she didn't finish her sentence and wouldn't look up at him, nor did she try to stop the tears from moistening his already damp shirt. "You just can't imagine what it's like to watch your children grow up and go away. Of course it has to happen, but I don't have to be happy about it, do I?" She looked up, still crying but beginning to smile, eyelashes fluttering, and Steve leaned over to kiss her on the forehead. His mother, all alone. He swallowed hard.

"I know it's been rough for you, Mom. With Vernon gone and everything." He felt her stiffen.

"Well, everyone makes choices," she retorted. Then she sniffed and wiped her nose with the back of her mud-stained hand. "Now, when do you start, and what's he paying you?"

Steve told her the sum he and Mr. Levine, the camp's owner, had agreed upon. "But that's with room and board," he felt compelled to add.

"Yes, I understand that," his mother said irritably. "You could probably get more elsewhere, but considering it's your first real job, and straight out of high school, it's not too bad. When I started butchering at the IGA in '43, I was making a good deal less than that."

"I think it's pretty standard pay."

"Well, be sure he doesn't work you to death. He's probably just like the rest of those city people, thinking your time isn't as valuable as theirs. I know you're conscientious, so don't break your back working."

He assured his mother he wouldn't, then awkwardly disengaged himself from her arm to go inside and pack.

"What's Carol Ann doing this summer?" she called, after the screen door had slapped shut, and he was almost inside his bedroom.

"I don't know."

"Isn't she working up there too? In the kitchen, I think."

"She didn't tell me," he yelled. "Where'd you hear that?"

"Just around." By the tone of his mother's voice, Steve could tell she was back in charge, pleased with herself for knowing something he didn't.

The maintenance crew and the kitchen staff ate meals together after the kids and counselors left the dining hall, a massive old building made of stone, cool in the worst heat, with a six-foot-high fireplace and mahogany-paneled walls. The place had once been a banker's estate, and then a fashionable resort in the twenties; now it played host to a hundred teenagers who were supposed to play instruments all summer long. It didn't sound like much of a vacation to Steve, but then again, he didn't see the kids do a whole lot more than laze around, smoke cigarettes and pot in their "secret" spot in the woods, and occasionally practice their scales.

Carol Ann, the assistant cook, pushed her plate of tuna fish and potato salad across the table. "Yuck. After having my hands in this stuff all morning, I can't stand to look at it." The fish-and-soy-bean mixture congealed in its oil, the salad swimming in a sea of artificial mayonnaise. She wiped her forehead with a napkin and lit a cigarette, apologizing to Steve with a shrug; everyone at the table was already smoking.

"Hey, Pinny! What are you going to do about those girls? Hell of a problem, huh?" said Dick, the chef, a Port Elizabeth local. He tugged at his beard with a lewd gesture, winking, and the whole table of staff laughed.

"Yes. What *are* you going to do?" echoed Carol Ann.

Steve concentrated on his food, embarrassed, his cheeks gathering heat. Two fifteen-year-old flute players, both named Lisa, had been following him everywhere. One was loud, one quiet, and although they pretended not to notice him, they shadowed him all day long.

"What am I supposed to do? I just do my work. I've never even talked to them. They ignore me, and I ignore them." He wondered if Carol Ann might be jealous, not that there was any reason for it. He watched her laugh with Dick about something, then concluded she was falling in love with the chef.

By summer's end, Steve had received two dozen notes in two different handwritings. The most recent one said:

Dear Steven Pinny,

You don't know me, and you probably think I'm too young for you, but I'm not. I hope I can see you after the summer, and I definitely want to come back next summer *as long as you do*. Don't forget me!

Love,
Lisa

He didn't tell anyone about the letters, knowing Dick and the others would think the whole thing the world's greatest joke, and Carol Ann would never let him forget it. But the notes touched him, somehow, and he felt curiously better for the first time since he'd learned he'd flunked the running trials. He let his hair grow long enough to graze his collar, and while shaving in the mornings after his run, he'd survey himself in the mirror, his sharp blue eyes and pointy nose (the image of Vernon's), and decide he couldn't be that bad to look at. Who would have ever thought the Deaf Mute would get love letters—and from two girls, no less. He began to whistle as he went about his task of trying to stay the camp's decay: fixing broken screens, patching battered rooftops, adjusting the inadequate plumbing, painting the peeling piano practice shacks in bright white so they wouldn't be so hidden among the evergreens. Steve had found used condoms behind the uprights, and had brushed over countless lovers' graffiti. Always the two Lisas huddled somewhere in the background, whispering, pretending they didn't see him.

The last day of camp he was in the water in cut-offs, disconnecting the sections of dock, swimming them up to the shore where he would later forklift them into dry storage. With all the pieces of the dock against the sandy beach, the lake looked as if it had been set free from its fetters and could finally breathe. The season was ending, returning the lake to the North Country people. Steve could hear the campers' tour buses gunning their engines as the drivers prepared for the seven-hour trip to Manhattan Island, a mythical, distant land. He heard his name called and turned to find the quiet Lisa standing beside a thick maple tree, where she must have been hiding all along. She was skinny and pale, round glasses dominating her small but intelligent face.

"Hello, there," he said, but she didn't respond.

"Why don't you come out here and talk to me?" He didn't know where he'd found such boldness. Perhaps because she would be leaving forever in five minutes, Steve put aside his fear. The girl walked slowly toward him, rubbing her eyes beneath the lenses. He could see she'd been crying. The buses honked three times in rapid succession, urging on the stragglers. The urgency of the noise must have emboldened her, for she ran to Steve and put her arms around him, crying, "I'm gonna miss you so much." She said it over and over, holding him tightly, his wet body sticking to her clothing. He didn't know what else to do but hug her back, which she responded to by squeezing him harder. He put his hands in her wispy brown hair and made her look up at him; mascara ran down her cheeks like a tattered spider web.

"It's too bad we didn't talk sooner," he said and began to laugh. Her face lit up, tears drying in their tracks.

"You mean it?"

"Sure." He stroked the hair behind her ear. "Don't you think it's silly how we've never said a word until two minutes before you have to catch your bus?"

Laughing hard, almost hysterically, she laced her fingers into his and stood on tiptoe, lips pursed. They kissed two or three times with the non-stop honking in the background. Then she ran up the hill, yelling, "Wait for me! Don't leave without me!" and turned once to wave madly at Steve, her streaked cheeks shining in the sun, the black teary trails incongruous above her ecstatic grin. "Goodbye Steve! See you next year!"

Carol Ann confessed to seeing the whole scene. That night in his cabin, after a wild summer's-end party for all the counselors and staff, Steve and Carol Ann lay in bed together. They had just made love, he for the first time, though Carol Ann, it turned out, had experience. He was curled on his side, his head resting on her ample breast; he had never felt so content in his life. While Carol Ann stroked his hair and kept sighing, he let his fingers travel the length of her, the soft white skin of her belly like never-touched moss, its warmth so inviting and comfortable. Anything he said would sound flat and insufficient, but he had to say something to acknowledge this great event.

"Boy. I mean, Carol Ann, you are amazing."

Her small, elegant mouth blew him a kiss. "I've been waiting for you forever—did you know that? Since elementary school." She started licking the side of his neck, which first gave him chills, and then made him grow hard again. They stayed up all night, and what most astonished Steve was how natural they were together, how Carol Ann was not ashamed of her largeness. She was luscious, sprawled across the bed like some queen from a fairy tale, her auburn hair a magic carpet against his cheek.

His mother was, in the end, right about Steve's not moving back to the house. He accepted Mr. Levine's proposal of a year-round caretaker position and drove by the farmhouse to tell Kay and gather his things. She just nodded matter-of-factly, and when he added that he'd probably be seeing a lot of Carol Ann from now on, she didn't act at all surprised.

Chapter Five

1968

On the TV screen, women wearing long printed skirts and beaded necklaces, trailing garlands of poppies, danced to music in a palm tree-lined park. Not fiddling or country, which Paul had grown up with at the York Ferry Fourth of July barbeques, but rock-and-roll, a booming electric guitar beat that shook the fan-like fronds on the trees. The park was somewhere in California; he wished he were there, a link in that chain of weaving bodies, their faces uplifted in bliss, an almost religious ecstasy which might have had to do with drugs but which Paul preferred to believe was a natural product of freedom from order and adults.

He sipped his Genesee Cream Ale and switched off the TV when the "Summer of Love—1967" retrospective had ended, and the newsman started reciting numbers of dead troops, numbers of men missing in action, the daily body count in a place he didn't bother to locate on the colored metal globe in the living room. Vernon had served in the Air Force, but Paul knew nothing about his father's experience. It was a weekday, and the rest of the family were eating dinner at his grandmother's. Paul had managed to plead summer-school homework, and his mother, impressed, gladly took the others to Eleanor's house to allow him silence in which to concentrate. Paul had never been much of a student, and the real reason for his desire to be alone was the case of beer he'd stolen that afternoon from behind the

York Ferry Inn. Thrusting his head back, he poured the remaining contents of the bottle straight down. Beer number five. His twin, sister, and mother would return by about 9 o'clock or so, making it necessary for Paul to drink one and one-third sixpacks per hour to finish the entire case. His math, at least, was good for something. He pictured each beer bottle as a signpost he needed to pass on a journey whose destination was some idyllic place, complete with palm trees, girls in flowers, and the rock-and-roll, which sounded so sensual he could almost caress the strands of music.

Without the television blaring, the Pinny farmhouse sat perfectly quiet in its cradle of valley, the nineteen acres of pasture stretching toward the low curtain of Madnan's Ridge to the west, Lake Champlain's bright blue visible in the east, his mother's gardens splashing the green landscape with multicolored vegetables and the brilliant yellow of sunflowers. Paul left the big window and followed the hall, stepping down when he passed into the addition; the farmhouse was like a rabbit hutch with new rooms added onto the original structure, one for the twins, one for Zoe Mae. ("A girl needs her privacy," Kay had said. Paul thought his sister's privilege clearly unfair.) The corridor sloped lakeward to the back bedrooms. He spied among his sister's things but found nothing of interest. Eleven-year-old Zoe Mae kept her room as neat as a military barracks, her favorite books stacked beside her bed. Underneath her pillow was the "hidden" flashlight, which everyone except Kay knew about, along with her two favorite books of the moment, *Harriet the Spy* and *The Long Secret*. Her bookcase was crammed with former favorites, which she still read constantly. If Zoe Mae liked a story, she would read it again and again until she could practically recite the words by heart. She often tried to keep the twins as captive audience, but they quickly grew tired of listening. At night, Zoe Mae read aloud to her imaginary sister, Ramona, who always remained attentive. After concluding there was nothing to distract him here, and no Ramona either, he shut her door carefully and leaned back to guzzle another Jenny Cream.

His body felt warm and fluid, like those hippies in California must have felt. He smiled and swayed his hips, bumping the walls in imitation of the dancers' movements as he made his way to the bathroom. Dancing and peeing at the same time, he misfired, and a puddle of urine formed on the floor. Oh, he felt good—a little sleepy, very content. He hoped to reach that same starry high that made the hippies' eyes flutter, but when he kneeled to wipe up the pee, a wave of nausea washed over him, and he fought the urge to vomit. After it passed, he stumbled out to his father's old toolshed, where Paul had established his hiding place for beer and other secrets.

A mirror in the shape of a jagged P, which someone had long ago given his father, lit the darkness with refracted sunlight, the Adirondack summer day still stretching on. Paul grinned at his reflection, and a sturdy round face returned the smile: big straight teeth and a head of thick curls, blue eyes with delicate lashes and amazingly acne-free skin. His build was still scrawny for thirteen, he thought, but consoled himself with the knowledge that everyone compared him to his brother Dean, his most charismatic sibling. Paul wondered what his father looked like now. Kay's only portrait of him was the U.S. Air Force shot of Vernon in his mechanic's fatigues, wrench in hand, a full-fledged acknowledgment of the camera in an expression that radiated pride, patience, even power. The picture, which hung in the living room so that it was the first thing one saw upon entering, was now twenty-five years old. It seemed Vernon had engineered all the family photographs, appearing in none.

Surveying the ratchets and wrenches strung across the pegboard like a line of falling dominoes, Paul ran his fingers down the workbench. Coffee cans brimmed with nails, screws, and greasy, unidentifiable objects his father had called thingamabobs. Paul thought it was a real name until his mother told him otherwise. Vernon Pinny, in Paul's dim memory, was a tall man in overalls who puttered in this room late at night, his hands in constant motion, his head bent to a task, fingernails black, one thumb permanently disfigured by a misplaced mallet blow. Paul was five when Vernon disappeared. The night before his father left for Canada, Paul and Joe fell asleep in Vernon's lap watching a TV special on the Royal Wedding of a month earlier. His mother had oohed and aahed, he remembered.

This shed, more than anyplace else on the property, had something of his father in it, some presence or spell, the smell of a man. Beneath a pile of dropcloths, the remaining beer glistened; he took two more bottles. The room oozed darkness, things hidden and silenced. Mildewed cartons lined the back wall, none of them labeled. Once he'd investigated the top layer, finding only old magazines, bills, meaningless scraps of paper. Someday, Paul promised himself, he'd go through all of them and find something important, some key to his father his mother had overlooked. Maybe there were other photographs, mementos of Vernon's years in the Air Force, a helmet or a pair of boots. Maybe a medal, a letter of commendation. There would be no war letters, since Vernon hadn't met Kay until afterward, when he came home with his two broken legs.

Down the Short Bay Road in front of the house, a motorcycle flew, chrome glinting. Paul imagined himself racing down the Lakeshore Drive with no shirt on, the wind cooling his back, a keg of beer waiting at Elbow Beach. Himself as hero, a group of girls and guys greeting his arrival, crowding him in a crush of awe. He finished a Jenny and grabbed another, making his way to the compost heap behind the kitchen. He thought he was clever by peeing directly into the pile, a gesture that would please his mother for its economy—life and death in a cycle and all that, blossoms growing from the dungheap. He was studying the ecosystem in school. Then he remembered Kay, in a flood of memory formerly suppressed, admonishing his father not to do that very thing. Urine killed things, she'd said. So Paul was destroying the heap of natural fertilizer beneath him, not supplementing it after all. He zipped up and pushed the thought away, letting the alcohol absorb it and all unpleasantness like a sponge expanding. He knew he was selfish to drink a whole case, to take all the pleasure for himself. Earlier he'd considered calling Kenny Heller, his best friend, to ask if he wanted to join him at the task, but had decided against it. Paul didn't want to share. He wanted to drink all of it, all by himself. Often he resented being a twin, being forced to split everything in two. Tonight was a test he'd devised, a personal code of honor: to conquer a case of Jenny single-handed without anybody knowing. "See, Mom, I *am* doing my homework," he said loudly and laughed.

Too bad he didn't have a cigarette, he thought suddenly, damning himself for not thinking ahead. He didn't like smoking cigarettes as much as smelling them. His father's Lucky Strikes had burned perpetually on edges of counters, remembered at the last possible moment, caught in mid-air, his magician father's sleight-of-hand.

Stealing the case had been easy. George Reiser, owner of the inn and Dean's father-in-law, was an old drunk who didn't get around to taking in his deliveries until after 9 in the morning. Paul had simply lifted a case off the top of the stack and hidden it in a nearby scrap wood pile, transporting the bottles in two separate trips on his bicycle, the beer out of sight in an IGA grocery bag. The summer school teacher had threatened to call his mother after Paul showed up an hour late, but he talked her out of it, claiming a flat tire had forced him to walk the full four miles. He smiled a lot, looked contrite, and told her repeatedly how sorry he was; could he stay after class and find out what he'd missed? She was a young woman from the college in Plattsburgh, not a local. She didn't call Kay after all.

Sun bathed Madnan's Valley in a last soft light of gold flecked with green. Paul remembered sitting on the porch at this exact time of evening and watching his father, shirtless beneath the faded blue overalls, as he tilled the garden with a spade. Sweat ran down his arms in muddy rivulets, and his sparse, straw-colored hair was matted to his head. He wore no hat, no garden gloves. He'd plant the spade in the loamy earth, jump on the metal edge to push it deeper, then pick up a mountain of soil and turn it over, inspecting the rich dirt with his work-callused fingers. Then he'd straighten up and start again. The process went on forever, and Kay's two garden plots loomed for miles in Paul's memory. The sun had fallen across Vernon's shoulders as it dipped behind the ridge, striping the furrows with elongated triangles of light, and darkness closed in swiftly after that. His mother gathered the twins to put them to bed. "No," his father had called. "Wait! Let me hold the youngest a while; you take the other one in." Paul and Joe had sat on either side of his mother all afternoon watching Vernon dig, drinking lemonade, and Joe had fallen asleep. Why didn't Vernon call him by his name? And why was Joe "the other one"? It didn't make sense, yet it suggested why Paul had always known, without understanding why, that his father preferred him in some odd way, that he was more interested in his youngest son. Paul was born second by a few minutes; his mother called him "the last boy." The last baby was Zoe Mae, who said she couldn't remember anything about their father. She had no memory of him at all.

Stealing beer from the inn became a habit. Paul couldn't believe how easy it was; anyone could have done it, but he saw no evidence that he had company in his thievery. Every morning he took the empties back, leaving them with the others behind the dumpster. He was depositing some bottles into the wooden Genesee crates when Eileen Reiser opened the back door and found him.

"Hey, Paul! What are you doing?"

"Oh, not much. Hi, Eileen. I, uh, found these empties on Route 22, so I thought I'd drop them off over here to let you leave them for the delivery guy and that way, you'd get the deposit."

"That's awfully generous of you, but if they're not ours in the first place, you could just take them to the IGA and get some pocket money." Eileen was a petite blonde girl with crazy, frizzy hair that reminded him of the dancing hippie women in California. She was smiling at him now (probably thinking he was a cute boy), so he figured she didn't suspect the theft.

"That's a good idea, but I'll just leave these here for now, 'cause I have to get home to water the garden before the sun gets too hot."

"You people really help each other out, don't you?" Eileen asked, braiding her waist-length hair to one side of her face, looking thoughtfully in the direction of the lake, which wasn't visible from the inn. The farmhouse was out of sight as well, tucked behind the rise where the burnt-out remains of a general store still stood.

"Pretty much. Even my dumb twin."

"Don't call him that. Joe's a sweet boy."

"He's so boring, though. He never wants to do anything."

"Still. I thought you all stuck together."

"Oh, we do. I'm just fooling. Gotta' go. See ya."

She waved at him before starting to heft the cases of Genesee and Budweiser bottles into the rear of the bar. Paul circled back, making a clean, graceful arc on his bike across the parking lot.

"Want some help with those?"

"Buddy, I've been lugging these things around since I was your age. Younger, even." She wiped her hands on a cloth apron and held them up for inspection. "See?" They were red and cracked with use, dry from years of rinsing glasses, even though she was just eighteen. Paul was impressed.

"I wish I worked here."

"You do? Why on earth would you?"

"Oh, it seems like fun."

She laughed, hoisting a case onto her hips, and didn't object when Paul followed her inside, a case under each arm. "It's a lot of things, but it's not fun." She propped the beer against the wall, leaning her body into it as she opened the cooler door. "It's hard, hard work. You looking for a job?" Her words trailed over her shoulder to Paul, who was thrilled to be standing behind a bar for the first time. The collection of colored bottles and gleaming silver spouts looked like flasks in an alchemist's laboratory. "My dad's been talking about hiring someone to do a little extra cleanup—sweeping, mopping, that kind of stuff. It's off the books, of course. How old are you, anyway?"

"Almost fourteen."

"Well, I'll ask him about it, okay? When he gets up. You sure you're interested? It's just for the season, you know. We always have more business now—all the summer people and their guests. Dad thinks the place should be cleaner. It's better for business, he says."

"Listen, Eileen. Tell your dad I definitely want to do it."

For a moment she looked him over, a glimmer of suspicion in her eyes. "You're awfully eager. I didn't think pushing a broom around sounded so glamorous."

They were back outside, and she cocked her head at the upstairs window, as if she'd heard her name called. "Come back tomorrow, and I'll let you know what he says."

Summer school ended in late July—he barely passed—and Paul's days acquired a new rhythm. Each morning he spent two hours sweeping and mopping the York Ferry Inn, and the rest of the day was his own. Joe watered the garden while Paul sampled the various liquors of his employer. Each day he poured something different into his canteen, mixed it with water, and drank the results at the beach in the afternoon. His friends assumed he was drinking water, and Paul liked to think this was partially true; he didn't like to lie unnecessarily. After a few close calls, he learned not to drink too much—never again a case in three hours!—so that he didn't stumble or appear noticeably altered. Gum disguised his breath, and no one ever said a word. With luck and a little maneuvering, he avoided having to offer his canteen when a friend was thirsty. Paul felt at peace when he drank; he could actually pinpoint the precise moment when the alcohol infused his blood with tranquility, flushing his entire body with a slow solution of contentment.

At Elbow Beach, girls from school congregated near him and his friends, everyone's towels overlapping, their transistors all tuned to the same SUNY Plattsburgh station that played the California music, the foreign names of the groups like the words of an incantation: Jefferson Airplane, Quicksilver Messenger Service, Grateful Dead, and his favorite, It's a Beautiful Day.

He swam out to the raft on his first school-free day and lay there a long time, absorbing the brilliant heat of the sun, which failed to warm his heart, nor would it slow his rapid pulse, now quickened by the plunge into Lake Champlain's icy waters. He remembered learning in science class how the heart instinctively speeds up when someone senses danger. The example had been a deer seeing a lion in the distance. This fear caused the blood to pump faster, which enabled the deer to run faster than it could normally, to run for its life. The adrenaline of survival, his teacher called it. His own heart beat that fast, as if he, too, were running for his life, stock still on the bobbing raft. But what was he afraid of? He could see no predator stalking his scent, no enemy lurking in shadows. Paul sat up and looked at the shore where his friends sprawled across blankets on the hard sand, some of the girls playing cards, one boy brazenly smoking a cigarette, the primary colors of their bathing suits like quilted patchwork under the deepening azure sky. Frieda, a farmgirl who was a twin herself and a year older than he, waved at him vigorously, waved him back to shore.

"Hey Paul! Paul Pinny! Paul Pinny!"

It sounded like a chant, the syllables meaningless in such rapid succession. He saw his metal canteen, half-full of the alcohol solution, catching the sun's rays like a beacon, awaiting him on the towel beside Frieda, and swam toward it.

Nighttime always drew him to the shed, his father's lingering presence like the invisible magnet of the North Pole. He went late, after everyone had fallen asleep. The only side effect of alcohol, as far as he could tell, was raging insomnia. Though he never had hangovers, Paul could rarely get to sleep before dawn, so he used the early morning hours, when Joe was snoring loud enough for them both, to mine the contents of his father's old boxes. The first few weren't interesting at all: financial records of the last several years, some blurry pictures of his siblings, tied with string, carefully dated. Why didn't his mother throw these away? He found a cracked bowling ball that said, "Vernon Pinny, Top Scorer, 1955-6" in gold script. This surprised him. He couldn't remember his father doing anything like bowling in the York County Bowling League. He always remembered his father alone: alone in a room, a field, even in the auto shop where his partner, Henry, always worked nearby. Paul discovered an old pair of Vernon's black-rimmed glasses, the lenses badly scratched. He tried them on and looked for his reflection in the jagged P, losing his balance immediately, dizzy from the magnification. He looked like a fish in a funhouse mirror, all bloated and wide. Was that how his father saw the world? As if from the inside of an aquarium? Probably not; Paul understood how prescription glasses were supposed to work. It was strange, though, to feel the heavy rims on his nose, to know that his mysterious father had worn them himself; they'd rested on his sharp cheekbones and circled behind his ears, framed the world his father knew. Paul pocketed the glasses, wondering again why his mother had not gotten rid of such useless things, although he was certainly pleased to have them. It seemed she had thrown nothing away.

All through August he worked his way toward the bottom of the pile, finding little of interest. There were documents about mortgages, paperwork from the York Ferry Garage, receipts, and business correspondence. The auto repair shop his father had made prosper for fifteen years was now defunct; Henry had failed to maintain Vernon's high standards, or that was how his mother explained it. Dean had quit his apprentice position after his father's disappearance. Paul sifted through inventory accounts, delivery notices from the Greyhound depot in Marysville. What could his mother be thinking to save all this junk? He kept looking. It was cold in the shed at night, so he always took a sweater, and had never gone barefoot after the first time, but still a chill settled upon him under the bare bulb, and when he caught a glimpse of his reflection, it was dim and chalky. Of course, he kept the curtains drawn tight so that no light would leak, curtains cut raggedly and sewn by his father from old Army blankets, now moth-eaten and tattered. Here, sometimes, he felt afraid, threatened by the cold close air, by the lingering presence of his absent father, the smell that never faded, although he knew this sensation was the reason for his visits. The shed was little used; Dean had built his own workshop where he lived with his wife close to town. Steve had never been inclined to putter around in here, always preferring to be outdoors, even on the coldest of days. Neither was his twin interested enough to investigate. And his mother stayed away, except for storing her garden tools, and to add a box to the pile each year. It was just Paul and his father in here, the jagged mirror and the lightbulb.

When the end of the season approached, Eileen told him they wouldn't need his help after one post-Labor Day cleanup. She would return to doing those tasks herself, and less frequently. "York Ferry people don't need their bars so clean," she told him. He couldn't tell if she was being sarcastic or not.

Paul worried about his alcohol supply getting cut off, but if he had the will, he would find a way, that's what his mother always said about solving problems. In his possession was a key to the inn, which he would have to return to Eileen. No one had ever said, however, that he couldn't make a copy. Without too much hesitation, he biked up to the hardware store in Port Elizabeth to have it done. (The hardware lady in York Ferry knew everyone and always tried to guess what kind of locks the keys were for.) He resolved to be cautious, to come early in the morning and never to take too much; no one need ever know.

One windy night late in October, Paul reached the last box. He trembled as he carried it to the workbench, imagining some lost treasure inside, some precious token of his father previously overlooked. Although he usually limited his drinking to daytime so that he was stable by dinner when he would see his mother, that night he took the canteen to the shed. The cement floor leaked cold upward through the soles of his sneakers, and the jacket over his sweater failed to keep him warm. Lighting the woodstove tempted him, but the risk of discovery was too great. His breath fogged the air before him, clouding the mirror's flecked surface. After a swig on the canteen, he set to undoing the flaps of the carton, its bottom green with mildew and icy to the touch.

Junk. Another box of junk. Blank York Ferry Garage invoices, a catalogue of General Motors standard transmission parts, and a collection of poorly focused black-and-white snapshots of an infant spread-eagled across the braided rug in the living room. "Dean, first-crawled, 1948" was printed on the back in a neat hand, each picture barely distinguishable from the one before it. There were birthday cards from Dean's first birthday and an envelope of recipes cut from the newspaper. When Paul lifted a *Time* magazine from 1946, it let fall an unsealed envelope. Inside was a yellow piece of paper covered with writing; it had to be his father's. His writing was narrow, at first staying well between the lines, but by the end of the page, the words overlapped and bled into the margins. Although many phrases had been crossed out, the letter seemed complete, awaiting only a signature. The date was Nov. 11, 1946. The address of the farmhouse was printed neatly in the corner of the envelope, but there was no addressee.

Irene,

I can't stop thinking about you no matter what I do. I've met
a nice girl who I'm going to marry tomorrow, but I can't get
you out of my head or out of my heart, and I'm thinking
tonight I should call off this thing with Kay and come back to
Antwerp. But I can't even send this letter. I do know, though,
that I didn't want to leave you that morning, how I knew even
before I stepped out your door that I'd never see your lovely
face again, and it was either going AWOL or leaving you, and
I left you, and I'll never forgive myself for losing you. Never
and never. What's that saying—we won the war but lost the
battle. I did lose you. Oh god, I did. I remember your shoul-
derblades, poking out from your sweet back like nubby wings,
the firmness of your stomach beneath my hand, how small
your palm was against mine, my fingertips overlapping yours
a full inch. Oh Irene, how could I have shielded you from the
Germans and their bombs? After surviving three years in the
room with no windows, you were given the air, then had it
taken from you. How could I believe in God after that? He
didn't protect you. I didn't either. I will never forgive God,
nor me.

                                                    Your,

Vernon needed only to sign it and send it. Paul read through
the cramped words again and felt confused, wanting for himself
the love his father harbored for this woman, this stranger. It was
obvious to Paul that Vernon had gone in search of her, so many
years later that even if she had survived the war, she probably
wouldn't care about Vernon anymore. She probably had a family of her own. How many children would she walk away from to
find Vernon? He felt his mother had been wronged, somehow,
by this previous love; it was an intimate act of treason on his father's part. Paul should have found one love letter in all these
boxes addressed to Kay and not some foreign girl who was probably dead.

"What the hell are you doing in here!"

His mother slammed the door behind her, wrapped in
Vernon's old overcoat, wearing his black rubber fishing boots as

if it were raining or muddy outside, but they were completely dry, dwarfing her short legs.

"What are you doing?" she repeated.

"I couldn't sleep, Mom. I just couldn't." He tried to measure her anger; she looked more worried than mad, a sign in his favor. "So I came in here to look around for a while."

Her gaze traveled the circumference of the room, noting his canteen, the open box, the magazine and piece of paper in his hand. The gray-blue of her irises and the whites of her eyes carried a strange soft light into the room. Her hair was loose and disheveled, an airy cumulus cloud encircling her head. "Paul, it's freezing in here." She bit her lip. "I haven't been in the shed for a long time. Not at night." She looked again at the workbench, its surface covered with papers. "What are you doing, going through all that junk?"

"Just looking."

"Find anything?"

"Nope." He didn't know what to do with the letter, so he kept it in his hand while returning things to the box.

"Come on, son. You can clean up tomorrow. You scared me half to death when I couldn't find you in the house."

"Well, what were you doing up?"

"Sweetie, that's what I asked you, remember?"

Paul grabbed his canteen and tried to appear nonchalant as he slipped the letter beneath the magazine.

"Come on. You'll catch cold out here."

She pushed him out the door in front of her, and as she switched off the light, the bulb sizzled and sputtered out. He heard her murmur, "It almost smells like him in here."

In the warm, well-lit living room, she took his face in her hands and examined him closely. (He tried not to exhale.) He was just her height now and growing still, so she wouldn't be able to look him eye-to-eye much longer.

"Paul, is there something you're not telling me?"

He shook his head.

"Something at school? Your grades? You can talk to me. I won't get mad."

"Nothing, Mom. Really."

"Well, I don't like this, you roaming around in the middle of the night." Now that they were safe inside, Kay had recovered her anger. "You scared the hell out of me, you know, when I looked into your room and you weren't there. And you weren't in the kitchen, or the bathroom. I got frantic. I just happened to glance out the window and saw a tiny bit of light coming from the shed. Oh Paul," she said, stroking his hair rapidly and hugging him hard. "It was very odd, because for a minute—no, a split second, maybe—it was like when your father was here, and he could never sleep either, and he used to stay out there till all hours. I thought he was back. Or that it was a long time ago, and all these years hadn't happened."

Paul could feel his mother's heart beating through Vernon's overcoat, pumping against his own chest, and he remembered the deer's adrenaline, and then he couldn't tell if it was his own blood racing, or his mother's, or both. He didn't try to struggle out of her embrace, as he often did, and she whispered, "You miss him, don't you?"

He couldn't speak, but he nodded yes, yes he did.

Then she spun him around, slapped his cheek once, harshly, stinging him, and pushed him away. "Now don't ever frighten me like that again," she demanded, still whispering but louder. "Do you understand!"

He didn't answer, and he didn't turn around but backed slowly toward his room, leaving her there in the center of the braided rug, empty-handed.

1969

Seattle
September 1

Dear Kay,

I'm here at the Veteran's Hospital after suffering a minor
heart attack. The doctors say I have "every chance at total re-
covery," so you have little reason to worry. But it has become
clear to me that you no longer care what happens. During the
last nine years I have begged and pleaded with you to contact
me, and you refuse. I can no longer write you these letters in
which I try so hard to be honest with myself and you.

In last week's Sunday paper I read about the opening of the
new interstate highway up through the North Country. I
imagine it will change York Ferry quite a bit, assuming there
is an exit there, and even without an exit. The Adirondack
Northway. It's a pretty name for a stretch of asphalt. In the ar-
ticle it said that within the first 24 hours of opening, there
were several accidents, including a car full of elderly church
women obliterated by a drunk driver. Naturally I thought of
your mother. This stems from paranoia, I think. After this
heart attack, I've been realizing how you never think you're
going to be that one statistic: one in a hundred, or a thousand, or the tiny percentage that fails, or the rare, rare case
that confounds all the doctors. It's always someone else, we
think. Antwerp was heavily bombed, but there were more in-
juries than fatalities. Irene was one in a handful to die. That's
why I feared for Eleanor when I read the story.

I'm tired, Kay. I do my job, and I go home. I check the mail
every single day. Now I will stop writing and wait for you.

Vernon

Chapter Six

1974

Autumn blew in warm and clean, with the lake and sky the same color blue all through October. Maple leaves turned red, the linden yellow, yet each day dawned not warm but hot. Old Mr. Morissey, owner of the Champlain Bar & Grill, fished the mouth of the Bouquet River every morning, early. He didn't trust the idea of Indian Summer. He told Dean, and every other curious passerby who stopped to check on his progress, that winter was waiting, pausing like a hawk before the kill, just on the other side of Madnan's Ridge. "You can bet on it," Mr. Morissey said. "Today's the last day of this unnatural sun. Tomorrow's time for longjohns, like we always wear at this late date."

Early in the month, Dean had seen a thin glaze of frost on the lawns and stubbled cornfields, like icing on a homemade cake, a dribble of white, but it melted before the day began. The feel of summer lingered and lingered as York Ferry baked in the ninety-degree heat. Saturday nights, the air smelled of barbeque and campfires instead of woodstove smoke and burning leaves. The high school kids kept driving with the tops down on their convertibles, and the radio d.j.'s in Plattsburgh kept playing the big summer hits, as if it were still July. The weather was on the tip of everyone's tongue, a bead waiting to fall.

"Dean, this house is too small for us," Cathy announced one Saturday morning. "I'm taking the kids to Glens Falls," she said, packing the children's things for a weekend at her sister's. Dean recalled their latest argument—something about money, of course—and stood by the station wagon as she loaded the car. Ignoring his offer of help, Cathy hustled the children to get in before the day got too hot and they missed too much time at Aunt Rose's swimming pool. Dean, Jr., and Sheila clung to their father's arms.

"Can't you come with us?" both asked.

"Sorry, kids." He buckled them in. "I've got to go to work to keep everybody in shoes. You have a good time." He kissed them each, once, locked the doors, and lowered his head to speak to Cathy, though they did not look at one another. "Drive carefully," he said. It sounded like an order.

She put the car in reverse. "I always do, Dean," she said, backing down the driveway. The kids waved until the car disappeared around a bend in the Bouquet. Dean got into his Jeep and drove off in the opposite direction.

On his way to road crew headquarters for York County, Dean tuned in the weather report. "More summer temperatures today and tomorrow, but we're looking for a break next week." The announcer started talking about low pressure areas and a Canadian cold front descending from up north; Dean turned the radio off. Barring an emergency, Saturday was an easy shift on the crew, where he was second in command. The next day would provide an opportunity for fishing, especially if the heat kept up. Usually he spent Sundays doing odd jobs at home or helping his mother at the farmhouse. Maybe he would ask Steve to join him at the river, or perhaps he would buy some homemade applejack from Mr. Morissey and spend the day by himself on the lake, being alone and quiet. For the last ten years he'd worked two jobs, first helping to support his mother, brothers, and sister after Vernon left, and later Cathy, then their two children. He was tired. Although he could now depend on his brothers to take care of themselves, and Kay had returned to work to support the farmhouse and Zoe Mae, Dean still faced payments on his Jeep, payments on the mortgage, payments on Cathy's car, and other miscellaneous payments. New bills each month added ballast to balances of old ones. The night before he and Cathy had argued over the price of tennis shoes. "Thirty-five bucks for sneakers? Jesus Christ!" he'd yelled. "You didn't tell me about this."

"They outgrow them so fast, Dean," Cathy responded. "The prices keep rising. I bought myself one pair on sale. And I *did* tell you."

He was angry at himself for losing his temper, raising his voice when he tried so hard to be the responsible man of reason. Every month when the bills came in, he had flashes of regret for his early marriage; he fantasized about driving north to Canada and not coming back. But his reverie ended at the border; he didn't know what he'd do with himself once he'd crossed over. And he didn't want to follow in his father's disappearing footsteps.

Late Saturday afternoon, after he'd showered off the highway dust and changed into clean, pressed jeans, he drove to Champlain's to eat. On the weekends, a local bluegrass band played there, and the dance floor would fill with teenagers and old people stomping their feet and clapping while the more daring couples sashayed down the center. Dean and Cathy used to dance there when they'd first started going together. On those summer nights he would toss blankets and pillows in the back of a borrowed county pickup and drive with her, after dancing, down a dirt road to where they could see Vermont flickering on the other side of the lake and watch the moon travel across the black sky. They made love, sleeping outside whenever it was warm enough, and the time passed quickly, evaporating like the morning mist off the water. In the fall she discovered she was pregnant, and they married immediately. In the spring, the child died inside her. Cathy was in the hospital for over a week; at the same time, York County laid Dean off for six months. It was the worst time he could remember since Vernon took off.

At Champlain's, the band was just beginning to set up in one corner of the huge dance floor. Only a few old men were in the place, the ones who'd been at the same spots at the bar all day, the vinyl stooltops molding around their skinny bottoms. Dean took a seat at one end of the horseshoe-shaped bar, close to the band and far enough from the old-timers so that he had only to nod and smile his greetings. One of the old men, a veteran like Vernon, kept putting his prosthetic arm around the waist of the waitress, who expertly disengaged herself. Dean watched the scene with an odd mixture of glee and disgust.

"What'll you have, Dean?" asked the bartender.

"Give me a draft, Rick." Dean swiveled to face him. "A large one."

Families began to fill the tables in the restaurant area, children running and playing tag on the empty wooden floor until their parents ordered them back to their tables. He knew almost everyone who entered by name, the rest by sight. Sometimes Dean brought Cathy here; they liked the Wednesday special with all you could eat, all the soda pop you could drink for $3 a head, only a buck for the kids. It had been several months since their last spaghetti outing, however, and he couldn't even remember when he'd last brought Cathy here for dinner without the children. They never went out with other couples; Cathy didn't care for most of his friends' wives. Her sisters were her closest confidantes. Dean spent a lot of time at Champlain's though, often arriving after work to have a beer or two with his buddies.

"You're looking clean tonight, Dean," said a man from the road crew who had just walked in with his girlfriend. "What's the occasion?"

"Nothing special. Just thought I'd play some pool and watch the dance floor."

"Come on and join us if you want, we're grabbing a table. Don't get yourself in trouble, now." He put his arm around his girlfriend's shoulder and winked at Dean before walking away.

At the bar Dean ate a cheeseburger and fries, both drowning

in ketchup, drank his beer slowly, and observed the crowd. He chatted with people who greeted him, ordered more beer, and studied the faces of those filing into Champlain's on the strange, summer-like night at the tail end of October. He liked being there without having to worry about arriving home at a particular time. He liked knowing that Cathy would not be there to harangue him; this knowledge filled him with a kind of leisure he hadn't experienced since childhood. Around nine o'clock, the band broke into a Virginia Reel, and an elderly couple, dressed in bright green matching pantsuits, started the dancing.

"Is that Dean? The admirable older brother?" It was Carol Ann, Steve's girlfriend. "We've got a camp reunion going on in back. Come and join us," she ordered, deftly handling the four pitchers of beer Rick had deposited on the bar. Carol Ann was a big woman, six feet tall, hair down to her waist, with a surprisingly soft manner. She was confident and sure of herself, comfortable in her bigness in a way Cathy would never be with her own petite size. Shy Steve had done pretty well for himself, Dean thought.

A dozen people crowded around the table, his brother not among them, all of whom he knew except for two. "Dean, this is Susan, who I worked with in the kitchen last summer. My able assistant cook." Carol Ann raised her beerglass to the rather plain girl, who nodded at him and looked away. "And next to you is Miriam, her roommate at Vermont University. She's from— where?—Israel? I picked them up at the ferry this afternoon. And you know everyone else." Carol Ann poured him a beer and returned to her conversation with Susan.

Miriam looked different from the women he knew: brown eyes so dark they seemed black, skin the color of scorched sand and a thick black braid that fell by her hips and moved from side to side as she spoke. Once he understood that she really was from Israel, he started asking questions. Did she live in the desert? Had she served in the army? He didn't know a lot about her country, only scattered information he'd gathered from the news, but he liked the idea that this girl beside him had come from so far a place and ended up in York Ferry, New York, drinking beer and smiling at him.

"What is your name again?" she asked with a slight accent.

"Dean. Dependable Dean, just like the commercial."

She didn't know what he was talking about.

"It's an advertisement for a car dealer up in P-burgh. 'Dean, Dean, DEPENDABLE Dean!'" He sang the jingle loudly, making her laugh. Miriam wore a half-dozen bracelets on each wrist; extravagant gestures accompanied all her words. The sound of the jewelry sliding up and down her arms kept floating in Dean's ears. He liked it, all that brass glittering in the dim light like sparks from a campfire. And her clothes, too—nothing a York Ferry girl would ever wear—a red dress the same color as his deer-hunting jacket. She tapped her lips with her forefinger as she contemplated what to say, and her thick eyebrows rose when she asked a question. She told him about picking grapefruit and avocados on the irrigated desert farms; she told him about the Dead Sea, which had so much salt you could float forever without effort; she told him about being a weapons clerk at a checkpoint on the enemy border.

Other members of the group danced and table-hopped, but the two of them paid little attention. He told Miriam about his large family, about his wife and children, Vernon, his two jobs. She listened carefully, as if it were all very important information; sometimes she closed her eyes and wrapped the braid around her hand, as if to concentrate more intently. She didn't flinch when Dean mentioned Cathy, although later she asked why he didn't wear a wedding band. (He said it was a work hazard which might cause him to lose a finger to a saw.) Dean wanted her to play pool, but she said she didn't play. Miriam asked him to dance, but he said he didn't dance.

"How about I play pool with you, and then you dance with me. Okay?" She was already heading toward the pool table.

Explaining the rules, showing her how to hold the cue and set the balls, Dean watched her with desire: her dark, slender arms poised over the green felt, bracelets falling down to her wrists so that she had to keep pushing them up on her forearms. When he leaned over her shoulders to demonstrate a better approach to a shot, he could smell her perfume, a foreign scent. He imagined this was how the desert must smell at the edge of an oasis. He was aware of the stares from the bar, the eyes at his back, a growing attention paid to him and the stranger. Miriam didn't notice the particular curiosity she was arousing, the kind any stranger would receive in York Ferry at any time, but especially on a Saturday night at Champlain's when half the town was there minding the other half's business. Dean's behavior toward her was duly noted, he was sure. Miriam concentrated on her game, and she wasn't half bad for a beginner. After losing twice, she reminded Dean of his promise.

"I really can't dance," he insisted. "It's been years."

"Yes, but we made a deal. Come on." She lay the cue down and preceded him onto the dance floor, which was much emptier than it had been earlier.

The music boomed, guitars and banjos twanging out from speakers beside the band. It was too loud for conversation so they just grinned at each other, dancing, Dean slowly at first, embarrassed that his six-foot solid body was too big and clumsy to be traveling across a dance floor.

It was dangerous to be out there with her. A circle of children were the only other bodies dancing. Miriam kept smiling, moving in a sinuous circle around him, not the typical York Ferry do-si-do, and he couldn't make himself stop her, or leave. He swayed his hips and kept his eyes on hers. For ten long minutes he ignored the looks he knew were directed their way, and as they passed in front of a window, he was distracted by their reflection; he felt separate from himself, distanced from his actions. The image of himself and the exotic young woman excited him.

When the band took a break, they returned to the table to get a drink, both of them flushed and sweating. Dean suggested they go outside, and she followed him out a rear door, past the parking lot, to where they could see the moon shining down on a meadow that lay at the base of Madnan's Ridge. They stood side by side in the still air, listening to the rasp of a bullfrog which sounded distantly from the direction of the lake. Laughter and voices drifted out from the bar; a man shouted that he had tilted the pinball machine.

"I like this part of the country," Miriam said. "How it looks and smells and the people, too. I've been treated well here."

The moonlight was bright, illuminating a farm beneath the ridge and a small grove of pines just beside it. Dean saw something move by the trees. "Look over there," he whispered. "A buck. A four-pointer, I think."

She couldn't see it.

"Just to the left of those pines, out in the open. Standing still." He put a hand on her elbow and pointed with the other.

When she saw the deer she gasped. "I've never seen one before! He's so graceful."

Dean stepped behind her and put his arms around her waist, holding her the way he'd wanted to on the dance floor but hadn't dared. She remained perfectly still, and they stood there quietly, watching the deer until it walked slowly back into the trees. Miriam turned around in the circle of his arms to face him. Her hands were clasped in front of her, and she was not smiling. She had to look up, since he was almost a foot taller than she.

"I've had a wonderful time tonight. You are a very nice man. I should go back to Susan now. And you, you'll go home?"

"I guess." He didn't want to let go of her, and she didn't seem anxious to move so they stayed like that for another long while, not talking, just looking at one another, a chorus of crickets filling the silence. Finally, he asked, "Want to go to the lake? We could build a fire on the shore. It's real pretty out there."

She stepped back from him and turned to where they'd seen

the deer. She saw only moonlight now, silver, shining hard on the meadow. The tip of her braid went up to her lips. "I used to chew on my pigtail when I was little. Now I only do it when I can't make up my mind." She let go of the hair. "This is not wise. For you or for me."

Dean looked over at his Jeep at the far end of the lot. He could get in it, drive home and go to bed, safe and proper, as he always had year after year since his marriage. Or he could drive away with Miriam. Somewhere. He didn't want to say good-bye to her yet. "It's definitely not wise," he agreed. "Let's do it anyway."

They built a small fire on a hidden cove of the lakeshore. Technically they were trespassing, but Dean knew the owners of the property were away for the winter. No one would see them there. The water was calm except for the occasional splash of a fish as he spread out a blanket he kept in the Jeep for the kids. While the fire hissed and crackled, he told Miriam the names of all the mountains they could see: Hangman's Peak, Goat Hill, Madnan's Mountain. They sat close but apart and Dean wanted badly to put his hand in her black hair, when a screaming whistle blasted the silence. Miriam jumped to her feet.

"What was that?"

"Relax." He laughed. "It's the night freight going up to Montreal. Look over there." He pointed south to a crook in the low mountains; a chain of red lights came into view, making an arc toward them, then disappeared. She remained standing, searching for the train. "You can't see it anymore from here," he said, the freight whistle still sounding. "It's gone."

"Like magic," she said, taking the hand he held out to her and sitting beside him, hips touching. She examined the bumps and ridges on his palms and fingertips, the badges of his long career spent hauling and digging. "Your hands are so callused," she said. "How can you feel anything?"

Dean shrugged. "I don't even notice them anymore." He put

his fingers to her cheek as if in answer to a challenge. "I can still feel, though." He plunged his thick fingers into the loose hair by her temples, then caressed her braid. "Can I undo this?"

She nodded and faced the other way, sitting Indian style. He unwound the three strands and spread them in a fan across her back. "I can feel your hair. It's smooth as fur." Then he kissed her neck, and she turned back to face him. Dean felt as if he were moving in slow motion, as if he were outside his body watching the two of them on a movie screen. He closed his eyes against the bright white of the moon.

It was already warm when Dean awoke, the sun hanging in the eastern sky over Vermont's Green Mountains. It was good to be naked out in the air; strange, too, but he liked it, the dry breeze on his skin. He could see the ridges of Miriam's spine through the brown skin of her back, and he ran his tongue down the bone. She shivered and curled up tighter, reaching for an imaginary blanket. Dean shook the sand out of his flannel shirt and draped it over her. He had left his watch at home but judged it to be around 8 o'clock; they ought to go soon, because a Sunday fisherman might appear any moment, and she'd said she wanted to get the early ferry. But she looked so tranquil sleeping that he let her be. He felt calm, happier to wake up to a new day than he had in a long time. It was still Indian summer, as the weatherman had promised. Today would be the last day. He ran fast into the water and dove; it was so cold he had to shout. Standing waist-deep in the lake, his body a mass of goose bumps, howling at the coldness of the water, he felt completely revitalized.

"You're crazy, Dean," Miriam called. "Not dependable."

He swam farther out, to where only his head was above water, and pretended to drown, arms flailing. "Rescue me!"

She threw off the shirt and ran in naked, swimming a strong freestyle toward him. "You're saved," she said upon reaching him, and they hugged, skin hard with cold. She wrapped her legs around him, kissing his ears, licking the water from his face; he wanted to make love again, there, but he sensed that they would certainly be caught.

"We better get out of here," he said, reluctantly disentangling himself.

They dried each other off with the blanket, and then Dean took the closest road that led out of town. "Now, *this* is dangerous," he said as a car passed, and its driver waved. Dean had the only red Jeep in York Ferry. Miriam asked if she should try to hide, but he said it didn't matter. "That guy will just have something to add to whatever story's already going around."

The road wound through apple orchards and corn fields, past the church with a full parking lot, over the Bouquet, then out in the direction of the Northway. Miriam's hair dried in the wind, and Dean laughed to think what they must look like—as if they'd just stepped from the shower, she in her red dress in his red Jeep on a Sunday morning. Miriam laughed, too. "We are peanuts, yes?"

"Nuts," he corrected.

They stopped at a store in Whalen to buy something to eat, then drove up an old logging road that went almost to the top of Madnan's Ridge. At a small meadow he parked and proudly showed off the best view in the county. "You can see clear to Vermont University from here," he said, pointing. "There's that steeple in the center of Burlington."

Miriam located it, shielding her eyes from the sun, which was now directly overhead. They saw a ferry chart a path across the lake, so miniature in the distance it reminded Dean of his children's toy boats in the bathtub. "Today's the last day for the ferry," he said. "After that, you have to take the bridge down in Marysville to cross over. It's two or three hours from here to there."

She raised her eyebrows. "I don't think I'll be coming back. You have enough to think about."

"I guess so." Dean looked away.

After he'd cut the last of the apple with his pocket knife and Miriam had eaten her half, they sat together quietly. The wind had picked up, and the fir branches around their meadow rustled against one another, scraping limbs. She was watching a cluster of milkweed bushes lean toward them in the breeze. Some of the white tufts floated away, and she ran off, chasing them, returning with a handful. "Feel how soft this is! I've never seen this feathery plant." She rubbed the downy stuff across his cheeks and lips, then let it go. The wind caught hold of the matted milkweed and scattered it down the hillside. All of it disappeared. "It's getting cool," she said, wrapping her shawl tightly around her and resting her head on his shoulder. "I must get the last ferry." The sun was to the rear of their picnic spot now, almost fallen behind the mountains, casting their joined shadows onto the field.

Dean took back roads to the ferry landing, passing only a few farmhouses, which already had lights going and chimneys smoking. They were silent the whole ride, Dean wondering how to say good-bye, or what to say at all. They could hear the last-warning horn blowing as they approached the landing, so he drove directly to the ticket booth. Susan was waiting, frowning, two torn stubs in hand. Upon seeing Miriam, she tapped her watch and ran onto the boat.

"Well," he began, but Miriam shook her head.

"I have to go." She squeezed his fingers and rushed off, sandals slapping the pavement. The ticket collector frowned as she slipped by him while he swung the gate closed. "That's it," he called up to the ferry captain, but just then a man on a bicycle rode up, lifted the bike to his shoulders, and ran up the ramp, slipping and nearly falling into the lake. Miriam had evaporated into the crowd on deck.

"Goddamn college kids," the ticket man muttered.

Dean stood by the rail and scanned the faces for Miriam's, but it was getting hard to see in the twilight. A young family beside him waved at an elderly couple on deck, dabbing their faces with handkerchiefs, waving them in farewell. Finally he spotted her red dress. She was hugging her friend, not looking in his direction. "Good-bye!" Dean yelled as loud as he could; he knew she couldn't hear him. The ferry finished turning around and went forward, full speed, toward Vermont. A series of waves slammed against the wooden pilings below him.

When Dean pulled into the driveway, Cathy's Buick was there and unpacked. The whole house was lit, and he could hear them scurrying around inside. He was cold from the ride and decided it was time to put the top on the Jeep. From the back door, he saw the kids at the table sipping soup.

"Who's been eating my soup?" he growled as he came up behind his daughter's chair.

"Daddy's here!"

The boy and girl got up to hug him. They were still light enough that he could pick one up in each arm. "Did you have fun at Aunt Rose's? Where's your mother?"

Cathy came in from the living room, cigarette in one hand, coffee cup in the other. "Hi, Dean. We just got in."

He put the children down and went to her, kissing her cheek slowly, pausing there with his lips against her skin. She turned away. "So, you're not still mad about the shoes, huh?"

"Forget the shoes." He shook his head. "I'm sorry for losing my temper."

"Kids! Back to the table." She walked toward the stove, stopping to collect an empty bowl from the cupboard. "Eat your soup while it's hot," she called. "Want some, Dean?"

At the table he sat beside her, remembering how they used to hold hands when they'd just married. Cathy studied his face, watched him watching the children. He kept nodding, turning around to take in the whole kitchen and the darkness outside. "It's back to the old routine," he said with a contented half-smile. "I bet there'll be frost tomorrow. Remind me to put the top on the Jeep tonight."

Dean reached over to smooth Sheila's hair and then to wipe

some tomato soup from his son's mouth with a napkin. "How was your sister's? Car run all right?"

"Rose was fine, but you know she drives me crazy after a while. She can be awfully snotty with that wealthy husband of hers. And the car ran fine." Cathy drummed her fingers on the tabletop, tapping her foot rapidly.

Finally, Dean reached over and took her hand. She looked at him open-mouthed, gathering her words, but he spoke first. "I'm glad you're all back," he said, sandwiching her palm between his. "Come on, kids, help me get some firewood, and we'll get the stove going."

The dead leaves fell from the trees and blanketed the earth, so that, within a week, Indian Summer was nearly forgotten. Mr. Morissey sold his homemade applejack with a vengeance. Among his steady customers, Dean seemed to be the only York Ferry resident having trouble adjusting to the long-delayed winter season. No matter how many layers he wore, Dean couldn't stop fighting a chill. Every time he visited Mr. Morissey for a new half-gallon of the sweet, potent drink, the old man warned him, "It's gonna get a lot colder yet, boy. This ain't nothing."

Chapter Seven

Dean decided to look for that girl despite their decision not to see each other again. He was shaving at four in the morning when it came to him, the certainty of seeing her angular face, her ebony hair. He heard Cathy mumble in her sleep, reach for him to find only air, then grab the clock instead.

"Thought you had today off, Dean," she said, her normally quick voice still thick with sleep.

"Yeah, thought I did too. It's next week I get Thursday off." He spoke softly so as not to wake Dean, Jr., and Sheila, who slept peacefully, he hoped, in the other bedroom. Actually he did have the day free. After his morning job, delivering produce to a dozen markets in Plattsburgh, he usually had an hour before he had to report to county headquarters for the road crew's afternoon shift. Yesterday his crew boss told him to get some rest instead of showing up on site the next day; Dean had a lot of time coming to him, he said. Overtime on the crew paid well. Dean had worked as late as midnight on emergency jobs; more than once he'd been out until morning.

"Should I fix you some lunch?" Cathy asked. Her short blonde hair tumbled over the pillows.

"I'll get something in P-burgh. That's all right," he said. "Might be home late tonight if we're still having trouble with those guardrails on Route 22. They're a bitch to put into that frozen ground."

Dean couldn't tell whether Cathy suspected he was preparing for a lie. The details were true enough; he *had* been working Route 22 the day before. But he would be in Vermont tonight, he hoped, and Cathy would never know the difference. She turned onto her side, said, "See you later, then," and began breathing heavily, as if she'd fallen asleep right away. But her hands were clenching the blankets. He patted her hip and left, descending the stairs on tiptoe. He didn't like to kiss his children good-bye in the morning because often they woke up and asked him to stay home with them. He always had to say, "No, I'm sorry I can't," and sometimes his son would cry, sometimes Sheila, and occasionally both would wail at full tilt, prompting Cathy to yell: "Goddamnit! Can't you just leave for work like other men do without making a scene?"

He took his lined denim jacket from the rack, looking himself up and down in the full-length mirror behind the door. He knew he was in pretty good shape: his torso tight from lifting, digging, his broad body taut. During the last month, the exact amount of time since he met Miriam, he'd stayed away from the bars, worked hard, tried to get along with Cathy. There was some gray in the dark hair which unfurled over his forehead, some lines of permanent worry etched across his brow. "Twenty-seven years old, and an old man," Dean's boss liked to say of him. But it wasn't quite true. Not yet.

He left Plattsburgh Produce at nine, carrying two different kinds of avocados in a paper sack. He planned to drive around York Ferry on back roads into Marysville, where he would pick up the bridge and flee his home grounds for the day. First, he had to track down Carol Ann to see if she had Miriam's number. He dialed the music camp's telephone from a booth outside of Plattsburgh, predicting Carol Ann would give him a hard time about what he was doing, cheating in plain sight. She'd lecture him for a while, but she'd give in.

"Dean? This is a surprise. What are you doing out of work in the middle of the day?" Carol Ann had recently been laid off by the uniform factory, which had supported nearby Port Elizabeth for as long as anyone could remember. The owners had shut the plant down in favor of the far cheaper labor available outside the United States. Dean was glad none of his family had ever worked there.

"I need to ask a favor of favorite brother's favorite woman, and I'm hoping not to hear a whole lot of grief about it, okay?" He said he was at her mercy.

She listened to his request and then fumbled for her address book. She didn't even attempt to talk him out of it. All she said was, "This is Susan's dormitory, and I'm ninety-nine percent positive they share a room. Try this number."

He took off whistling. Carol Ann was a prize, he thought.

His red Jeep reflected the low November sun as he sped along the very highway he'd mentioned earlier to his wife. Lake Champlain glistened between him and Vermont, between his body and Miriam's, the dark foreign girl whose tongue had explored him eagerly, without shyness or shame. The lake today sparkled smooth and supple; he wished he could dive in and swim across instead of patiently traveling so far south to the bridge, only to travel the same distance north once he reached Vermont.

Marysville was York County's largest town. It had an Amtrak station and a Northway ramp as well as the bridge, so it had more traffic than anyplace else in the region except Plattsburgh. Even so, he knew his red Jeep was conspicuous; most men he knew drove big Fords or Chevrolets or jacked-up pickups. Dean's shining vehicle was now attracting some attention from a group of men wearing bright orange vests who were blocking the northbound lane so that they could plant guardrails where a handful had been ripped out of the ground by a drunk driving accident. Dean cursed himself for being so stupid. Of course he would have to slow down to talk; there were no cars behind him.

"Hey, Pinny. Thought I told you to stay home today," called Joe White, the crew boss, who was smoking a cigarette, watching three men struggle with shovels around an uprooted post. "Just can't keep the man away," he said to one of the crew. "Now that's a good worker. Dean Pinny'll be in *my* shoes one of these days, watching *you* dig holes."

"Sorry, Joe. I didn't actually come to work on my day off. I'm not that kind of asshole," said Dean, and the men laughed. Sometimes he felt uncomfortable with the way White was so obviously preparing him for the foreman's position when White moved on into administration. Dean often sensed the other men's resentment. "I need a new water pump for the Jeep, and they got nothing in P-burgh, so they sent me over to Burlington. There's a big dealership over there."

"Bet your wife's real pleased you're spending your first day off in three weeks chasing after *car parts* across the lake." Joe leered at him, saying "car parts" as if they were a section of female anatomy. Dean wondered if Joe had heard about Miriam; there was no privacy in York Ferry, not one iota.

"You kidding? She doesn't like me messing up the house all day, and anyway..." Just then a string of cars slowed behind him, and the two roadmen with walkie-talkies decided to wave Dean and his train on through.

"You be careful, Pinny," Joe shouted, and waved, his sly grin mocking Dean from the rear-view mirror.

He sped up, frustration bearing down on the gas pedal. It was impossible to have an affair in a small town, he thought, then laughed. An affair—Jesus! Is that what he was having? Driving two and a half hours to search for Miriam meant something significant; it wasn't just a casual screw of the kind his buddies often engaged in when they went drinking for whole weekends up in Plattsburgh.

After he paid his toll, the ticket woman handed him a green stub, which he tossed on the passenger seat, then reconsidered and dropped it out the window, where it fluttered briefly before falling to the water.

Somehow, Vermont still had its leaves, and the reds and yellow rustled brighter, more vibrantly than the foliage in New York's North Country. Maybe it was just because he was somewhere else that things looked better. Vergennes, Vermont, which he was passing through now, wasn't all that different from York Ferry, but it seemed another country; no one knew him here. He didn't know how to pronounce the name of the town, and he was surprised at the number of imported cars on the road. It was clear that there was more money in Vermont, and it didn't belong only to the summer people. Antique stores and sweater shops dotted the main street, and he saw a bookstore, a real estate agency or two, and a place selling only goods made in Vermont. Dean had lived his whole life just across the lake, but he could count on one hand the trips he'd made over that bridge; he'd never once been on the ferry. Neither, as far as he could remember, had any of his brothers, mother, or sister.

Before reaching Burlington proper, he stopped in a gas station for directions and spent a few minutes combing his unruly hair in the chipped rest room mirror. He wore a yellow sweater over his flannel shirt, and his jeans were without stain, still holding the crease from Cathy's iron. He'd scrubbed his fingernails that morning and washed his hair twice. "I look all right, I guess," he said aloud. "She liked me last time, anyway."

He found the address without difficulty, carried his sack of avocados up the four flights of stairs, and not until he'd waited five minutes did it occur to him that she might not be around that day; she might not want to see him even if she were available. His watch read 11:30; he hoped she'd be back for lunch.

A piece of paper was taped to the door, and a pencil dangled from a string. Someone had printed MESSAGES PLEASE in red block letters. He wrote: "Dean's in town. Guess which avacadoe is from Florida, which from California." Then he drew two diverging arrows and placed one fruit at each end of the doorway. He surveyed his handwriting, judging it passable but none too neat.

An hour later, he returned to find the door open, the fruit gone. Standing in the hall, he watched Miriam and Susan awhile before knocking on the jamb. Miriam's black hair was wet, and he could smell her skin—cool and scented, as exotic as passion fruit. She was dwarfed by a loose denim shirt over blue jeans. He thought she looked more American this time, not like when they met, but she still displayed her collection of bracelets, which jingled in accompaniment to her words, and her walnut-colored eyes flashed with pleasure as she recounted something to her roommate that Dean couldn't quite hear.

"Hey there," he said, knocking, and the two women turned from their desks to look up; he was almost as tall as the door frame.

Miriam selected the rough-skinned avocado from her windowsill and said, "Florida, right?"

Dean shook his head, grinning. "You still have them backward."

"I don't think so," she said, and invited him in, introducing him to Susan, who said she remembered him from York Ferry. Dean thought she surveyed him disapprovingly before returning to her book.

He and Miriam had the avocado argument the night they'd spent together at the lake. She said she'd picked avocados on a farm one summer, and she was positive that the California fruit was exactly like the Israeli kind. Dean, having handled produce for the last seven years, said no, the smooth-skinned Florida ones were closer to the imports. They hadn't really argued, of course; it was just the kind of comfortable disagreement he'd never have with Cathy, about something funny and odd and worth getting right even if it weren't important to their daily lives.

Miriam gestured for him to sit down on her bed. He felt too big for the room, but she continued to smile, completely at ease. He explained his mission with the Jeep, this time saying that there was a fellow with Jeep parts who lived in the countryside, and Dean was planning to drive out there this afternoon; that's what had brought him to Vermont. Would she like to join him?

Now she was nervous, running her fingers through her wavy

hair, biting the tip of a narrow braid which began at her left temple. "I do want to go," she said, first looking at him, then at her roommate, who was pretending to read a thick textbook, "I have classes this afternoon, but …"

Susan lit a cigarette, shaking the match out vehemently.

Dean stood up, brushing his palms on the thighs of his jeans. "That's all right. I was just passing through, anyway. If you're busy…"

"No. I'm coming with you. Let me get my jacket."

They walked down the steep hill to the center of town to have lunch before setting out. She put her arm through his and looked up tentatively. "Is this all right? You don't know anyone here, and neither do I." She stopped walking. "Why did you come?"

"I had to," he answered automatically.

"Well, I'm glad. Actually, I'm very glad. I hadn't stopped thinking about you and our weekend. Susan says it isn't right, though. She's told me stories about her adulterous father, who she says ruined her family."

"I'm not an adulterous father, though. I've never done this before."

She directed him to a busy bar where they ordered burgers and beer. So many people, all strangers, and he and Miriam could simply sit together, hands intertwined on the tabletop, and no one paid them any attention.

She studied him a long, silent while. He wanted to turn from the intensity of her gaze, but finally she closed her eyes, shaking her head and murmuring, "I don't know why I thought we could just spend that one night together and it would be over."

"I hadn't planned to see you until this morning when I was getting ready for work. I didn't even consider that you might not want to be with me." Dean felt so free with her, a woman he'd spent less than twenty-four hours with. Her foreignness and unfamiliar features invited him to be someone new, to rid himself of the baggage of Dean Caleb Pinny—husband, son, father, wage-earner, and fix-it man.

"I like you, Dean," she said, kissing the tip of his forefinger.

Their food arrived, and both of them ate voraciously, guzzling their beer, dousing their fries in a sea of ketchup. Dean felt like a teenager, unencumbered and happy, the way he had before Vernon had left the family, when they all took everything for granted, and no one said any different. Miriam said what she felt. "I like you, Dean." Just like that. When had anyone given him that kind of open, loving honesty? He knew his children loved him, his family, and he loved them in return. But that was different from the way Miriam reacted to him: wanting, hungry. He and Cathy now tolerated each other more than anything else. They talked about the children, or town gossip, or argued about money. They didn't discuss one another or how they felt. He couldn't remember if they ever had.

"Listen, Mister Dean," Miriam said as they walked back up the hill to where he'd parked the Jeep. "I need to tell you something about me that I didn't mention before because it didn't matter. But now that we're together more than once, I think it's important."

Immediate dread passed through him; did she have some kind of contagious disease? Then he felt ashamed.

"I didn't tell you I am—what do you call it? affianced?— engaged, to a man at home, whom I love very much."

Dean's hopes for the day ahead sank. "Will you still come with me?"

Miriam turned around to look at Lake Champlain and the distant Adirondacks, then pressed her eyes shut as if making a wish. "Yes."

They passed a white house with red hunting jackets and shirts strung across the porch like carnival streamers at the York County Fair. Miriam pointed at the clothing, then touched the outside of the Jeep. "Same color," she said, grinning gleefully.

They held hands when he wasn't shifting, and he was elated

that she'd disregarded her roommate's warnings, her classes, her boyfriend to spend the day with him. The smallest things delighted her: an old man waving as he crossed the street carrying a pumpkin; the golden corona of an elm above a churchyard; a bushel of orange clothing hefted near a laundromat by a white-haired woman in overalls. He explained to her the workings of deer season, and she was appalled to discover that Dean himself hunted.

"It's not for sport," he said. "We eat them."

"But you delight in killing them. Why must you eat wild meat?" She was disgusted.

"We're not like the city people who come up here and make a party of it, drinking all the way and firing at each other in the woods, then discard everything but the head and horns. My wife uses every part of the carcass." Just as Dean said "wife," he knew he'd made a mistake. He'd wanted to convince Miriam of the virtues of hunting, and he was looking forward to the long discussion they would have, but now she was staring distractedly out the window, shaking her head and sighing. Her previous delight in him and her surroundings vanished into his bald acknowledgment of adultery.

"Damn it. I'm sorry, Miriam. I didn't mean to bring her up."

"It's one thing for me, here for a whole year, and my Aaron so far away. He is serving in the army now. We made some agreements before I left," she said, still not looking at him, "and we thought our bond or love or whatever you want to call it was strong enough to survive a year of absence, of being with other people. I still believe this. In my country, anything can happen at any time. But you—you have a wife of many years, and children. It's not the same. It's not right."

"How old are you anyway?" It hadn't occurred to him to ask before.

"I turn twenty in spring."

"Are you serious?" Dean had figured she was in her early twenties; she acted older than any nineteen-year-old he knew. "I didn't think you were so young."

"I'm not so young," she answered, offended. "Some of the American girls in my dormitory who are my age—now *they* are so young. But they are not important right now."

Dean saw a sign for a state park and drove in. They walked from the nearly empty parking lot into a wide brown field. "Listen," he whispered, his hunting senses alert to the rustle and scurry of deer in the adjacent woods. "If we stay very, very still, they'll come out here to graze." Then he sat down exactly where he was standing and raised his arms to her. "Sit with me."

Miriam, now towering over him, looked down at his outstretched arms, and something passed across her face that Dean couldn't identify—desire or pity or the love one has for a child—and she dropped into his lap.

Ten minutes later, three does walked from the trees and clustered at the far edge of the field, looking up at Dean and Miriam quite casually, then returning to continue their lunch of cold winter grass.

"This is wonderful," Miriam whispered into his ear, and he kissed her neck in response. They watched the deer for an hour while it grew dark. "How can you kill these beautiful animals?" she asked.

Dean told her that meat in York Ferry's one supermarket was outrageously expensive. "Besides, if we didn't hunt, these deer would starve."

She twisted her one slim braid around her forefinger, her body resting comfortably on Dean's lap while his legs fell asleep, and he defended hunting until he had exhausted his argument.

"Intellectually, I understand your reasoning," she said finally. "But personally, I cannot see how you can sit here with me today and admire their beauty, and tomorrow pick up a gun to kill them. This I don't understand."

It was like the avocados, Dean thought: they held directly opposing views, yet they could talk without hostility. He had never learned how to argue with Cathy.

By the time they left, night and freezing temperatures had descended on the field. Driving back to Burlington, Dean relished the touch of Miriam's hands on his thigh, a small presence which made him feel secure, wanted, and the inside of the Jeep was like the cockpit of a rocket as they sped down unlit lanes toward the city. Once, stopped at a red light in the center of a deserted town, they began a long kiss, and shortly, someone honked behind them. "Dean, the light's turned green," Miriam murmured. "He wants to get by."

"Let'm wait," he answered, and the car drove around, its driver shaking his fist. Dean felt pleased with himself.

At dinner, Miriam ordered for them both a dish he had never heard of—an omelette in a piecrust was how she described it—which Dean thought was odd and bland.

"It's called quiche," she said. "I think it's delicious."

He asked her to repeat the name, and she did.

"Quiche me," he whispered, pretending to be an old-time actor in those black-and-white detective movies he watched on late-night TV. In their dark corner of the restaurant where everyone spoke French, although it wasn't the same French he had heard in Quebec, Miriam curled closer to him in the booth, and they sucked each other's fingers when the waiters turned their backs.

"Let me ask you something," Dean said, emboldened from the wine she'd ordered. He never drank wine.

"What?"

"Forget it. It's a crazy idea."

"Ask. I can always say no." She brushed his cheek with her hand. "Or yes."

"What would you say to a motel?" He spoke very fast.

"Tonight?"

"Right now."

At the first motel they found, Dean signed them in as Joe and Josephine White of Alligator Pear Lane, using the name for avocado that some of his old customers in the produce stores still uttered from time to time. There were two full-size orange beds in the room, and Miriam stood just inside the door, surveying the place with a crooked half-smile. "I can't believe I'm doing this," she said. "It's something people do in American movies."

"You can still say no," Dean said, undoing the buttons on her jacket and then throwing it to the floor, his hands loose in her long hair, his strong fingers massaging her scalp. "Or yes."

She'd never been in a room with two double beds and couldn't decide which one to sleep on. She lay down on one, Dean on the other. "I want to use them both," she said, so they made love on each of them, Miriam's body as strong as he remembered, brown and lean and eager. She was everything Cathy was not: small-breasted, dark and narrow. Her desire for him made itself clear in her every gesture, kiss, caress. He could remember nothing so urgent or intense in his history with Cathy except at the very beginning when they were teenagers in the bed of a pickup, both exploring their nakedness for the first time. That was nine years ago, Dean thought, as he looked up into Miriam's eyes while she arched and curled, and he tried to stop himself from calculating how old Miriam would have been that year—a child.

By 2 a.m., she had drifted to sleep, her tawny legs scissored around his torso, trembling and twitching from her dreams. She was perfectly at home with his body, which continued to surprise him. Dean and Cathy never slept wrapped around one another but vigilantly guarded their sides of the bed. He was wide awake, thinking about later, when he would go home, and if there would be a next time after this time, about his wife, whom he did not love, and his children, whom he did. He could not imagine living without his son and daughter, deserting them as his father had deserted him, although he saw them infrequently because of his work schedule, and when he was with them for a few hours at a stretch, he grew impatient with their demands on him.

"Miriam." He stroked her hair, traced her collarbone with his callused fingertips. "Miriam, you can't sleep here. I'll take you home."

"What?" Her voice was fuzzy, and she gripped him even tighter between her legs. "You are kidding me, no?"

"I'll drive you back to the dorm, then I have to get home."

"You're going home at three in the morning?" She loosened her hold.

"Probably four by the time I get there."

"And what will you say to your wife?" Miriam had never asked Cathy's name.

"I'll just lie. I can't not go home at all."

"She'll know you've been with someone."

"I know. There's nothing I can do now. I'll tell her I've been drinking with some guys from work, and she'll know I'm lying. She'll accuse me of lying, and I'll have to say I'm telling her the truth."

"You admire deer but you kill them, too," Miriam whispered.

"What?"

"Nothing. Is this the same kind of lie as the Jeep parts?" She propped herself on an elbow and stared, not waiting for his answer. "Don't you love her? Didn't you ever?"

"I don't know anymore. Maybe I did. Now I just work and work so my kids can have a good life, so they can have some of the things I didn't when my brothers and sister and me were growing up." He paused, remembering how it was important to Cathy, and then to him, to dress their children in nice clothing, to have a respectable car and home, a life quite unlike the Pinny kids at the ramshackle farmhouse, all of them in overalls and hand-me-downs through adolescence. "My wife rags at me for not being home enough, or being home too much, for what I'm not doing, for what I'm doing. I never know if I'm doing the right thing. I think she doesn't even like being in the same room with me anymore."

"What happened after our weekend together?" Miriam asked.

For a while, after the night with Miriam, Dean reflected that he had been happier at home; he'd made a special effort to be more patient with Cathy and the kids. But Dean, Jr., and Sheila went to bed early, and he left before they woke, returned after they were asleep. That left only Saturday afternoons and Sundays for all of them to be together, and when he and Cathy were in the house at the same time for more than an hour, there was bound to be a fight. Over money, usually, or the way the other treated the kids: she thought he spoiled Sheila, and he thought she coddled Dean, Jr. It was better that he stayed away, he thought.

"When we have sex, she grits her teeth," he added. "I can hear it. Or when we *had* sex, I should say."

"I listen to you, and I am amazed. Did you ever think that maybe you're the problem instead of blaming everything on her? What gives pleasure in *her* life? How do you make love with her? I bet it was not like tonight, not slow and gentle and loving."

Dean considered. "Maybe. Maybe you're a little bit right. I'm not sure. She's not very gentle or loving to me. Not like you are."

She smiled. "But of course it is not the same. Aaron and I have been together for almost four years now, and we are not this kind of passionate. It's different when it's not new. I just cannot understand why you stay in a marriage when you both sound miserable."

"I have responsibilities, Miriam. You don't have any, except to yourself. I have a son and a daughter to think of, and Cathy doesn't work because I think she should stay home with them. If I didn't have two jobs, we'd be struggling all the time."

She kissed his shoulder, then bit it, hard. "So you never see the children, right? Or just on weekends."

"Well, that's the price, I guess. I want them to be comfortable. There's a lot of people in York Ferry on unemployment, people spending their kids' food money on beer. They're growing up in all that, and I want them to feel secure, to know their father's right there, supporting them, in a safe home with both parents in it."

"But don't you see?" She got up and began pacing, still naked, hands on her hips. "You're not really *in* it. Their home is not secure."

"But they think it's secure; that's what counts."

"Your children? Don't fool yourself. You think your daughter doesn't know that her mother's unhappy? That her parents can't stand each other? You think your son doesn't wonder why his parents never touch one another? Dean, you're blind. Children sense all these things."

"But they're happy when they're home with Cathy. And they like being with me on Sundays. I take them out to the lake or to my mother's and let Cathy go off and have some time alone. They have fun with me." Dean could hear the defensive edge in his voice. Miriam's insinuations insulted him. How could she know anything? "I'm not around enough for them to see us really fight or get ugly," he said. "I don't hit my wife or my kids, like a lot of guys I know."

Pacing, Miriam clenched her fists in exasperation. "If you could hear how you sound, Dean. It's like you're divorced already. You're an absent father. My father was like that, always working, always looking out for the good of our country. I never knew him. I don't know him now."

"Hey, come over here." Dean sat on the edge of the bed and pulled her between his knees. Their eyes were almost level, and he linked his hands behind her buttocks. "I know you mean well, and you're very sweet, but you can't understand what it's like to be in a long marriage in a small town, with two kids and a father-in-law who can't keep his mouth shut, especially when he's drunk, which is always, and the whole town ends up at his bar. Everyone knows your business in York Ferry. You don't just go around getting divorces like they do in big cities. It just doesn't happen."

She squirmed out of his grasp. "If you don't want to get divorced, why don't you fix up your marriage? Make it better. Make it work. Sleeping around isn't going to fix anything."

"It's late." Dean began to dress. "I'll take you home."

She insisted that he dress her, which he did, reluctantly, and waves of guilt washed over him as he thought about the times he'd dressed his children, the way they waited for him to pull arms through sleeves, sleepy and trusting, as Miriam was now. He shuddered to think what they would make of all this. Dean and Miriam drove to the dormitory in silence. Burlington had shut down for the night; a bank clock flashed 3:26 a.m. and 25 degrees. It would be a long, cold ride back to New York.

Parked in front of her building, Dean considered switching off the engine, then decided against it. Miriam looked angry, and he thought she wasn't being fair.

"You're cheating on this Aaron person just like I'm lying to my wife. It's the same thing."

She didn't respond.

"You act so holy or something, like you know all about love and what everything means, what it's like to be a father, but you don't know. How can you know anything at nineteen?"

"I wish you wouldn't say my age like you were accusing me of something. I can't help how old I am."

Dean offered his hand in truce, which she tentatively accepted. He kissed her cheek. "I better get going. I'll have to change my clothes and head straight for P-burgh Produce. And maybe I'll bring you some asparagus next time to argue about."

She smiled, perhaps in spite of herself. "We didn't argue about the avocados. I know I'm right." She opened the door. "So, there's a next time?"

"I don't know. What do you think?"

Miriam rubbed her eyes. "It's very complicated."

Dean wished she would close the door; bone-chilling air was sweeping into the Jeep.

"You know," she said, kissing the hand she still held, then stepping outside, "I'm pretty lonely here."

"There's a next time, then, yes?"

"Or no," she said, and shut the door.

Dean backed out to the cross-street and sped homeward to York Ferry, where he shaved and put on a clean shirt while his wife pretended to be asleep. As he crept down the stairs to leave, he heard Sheila say to her brother, "Was that Daddy?" and Dean, Jr., said, "I didn't hear anything."

Chapter Eight

1975

Zoe Mae announced her decision to join the Coast Guard the night she graduated from high school. She said she wasn't the type to sit around York Ferry forever, drink too much, and get fat. Dean just snorted and rolled his eyes; Zoe Mae always had outrageous ideas. She'd never seen the ocean or any body of water bigger than Lake Champlain. Which was big, but no ocean. She was, however, nearly amphibious, having spent every summer of her life immersed in the chilled blue waters of the lake. The most peculiar part of Zoe Mae's plan was that she'd never been in a boat bigger than a canoe, not even the ferries whose wakes crisscrossed the New York-Vermont borders during the tourist season. Dean watched his mother's eyes widen with fear at Zoe Mae's pronouncement.

"I'd worry about her terribly," whispered Kay, digging her stubby fingernails into Dean's forearm. "Please try to talk her out of it. She won't listen to me."

He showed up late the next day, alone, and sat in his Jeep for a few minutes, watching Zoe Mae straddled on the porch rail, slurping from a bottle of soda. She acknowledged his presence with a nod but said nothing, staring out toward the lake with a contented smile, her short legs tapping the white wooden rails from time to time. Dean took the steps three at once, plotting his big-brother strategy.

"Hey, little girl." He pretended to hug her but instead locked her waist firmly in his right arm and lifted her up, making tough Zoe Mae dangle in the air like a hooked fish. "Let's you and me take a drive on the lakeshore. What do you say, sister?"

She went limp, so that the hundred or so pounds of her athlete's body hung on him as heavily as possible. Her whole life her brothers had been picking her up, and Zoe Mae had learned that dead weight was the most effective resistance.

"Yes, sir," she answered in military fashion, her face turning blood red from the upside-down position. "You aiming to carry me there like this?" She tapped the tips of her cowboy boots together as if she were perfectly comfortable. Dean set her down, and she swallowed the last of her drink. "You're so rude, Dean. You know that?" Her freckle-lipped smile flashed in the late afternoon sunlight, which filled Madnan's Valley with a lush green glow.

"Yeah, but at least I'm not going to do some dumb-ass thing like pledge ten years of my life to the Navy."

"It's six years, and the Coast Guard is much cooler than the Navy. I know. I read all the pamphlets."

Dean looked her over, already frustrated. "Go for a ride?" He pointed to his Jeep, figuring she would be a more pliable listener if she were away from the farmhouse, where the twins and Kay might be listening. Zoe Mae prided herself on being more stubborn than all the Pinnys put together; mostly she was obstinate on principle rather than because she believed in whatever she was arguing for. Dean assumed he still had a chance to talk reason.

"So, where's your famous boyfriend? Looks like a fine night for cruising up to P-burgh. I hear there's a new movie at the Adam & Eve Theater." He loved to rile her. On a dare, Zoe Mae and some friends had gone to the porno movie house near the Air Force base and laughed loudly during the entire film, whooping and annoying the other patrons, one of whom was Joe White who had passed on this information to Dean.

"Eric is *not* my boyfriend," she shouted and punched his shoulder. "And I'm not so sleazy as to go sleep in cheap motel rooms like you do." Her green eyes blazed. "Or as you're rumored to do." She amended her point, but Dean knew he'd been collared.

"I am the most responsible man in York Ferry, New York, and I was out making money to feed your big mouth when I should've been out screwing around." She could always turn things around so that he'd end up on the defensive. "Don't you go giving me a hard time, little one. You've been spending your days in the lap of luxury. C'mon."

He took her by the elbow, and she let herself be pulled toward the Jeep, dragging her feet like a kid.

"Hey, Mom!" she yelled at the kitchen window. "Me and Dean are driving up to P-burgh. He's going to initiate me in a life of crime! Don't hold dinner."

He had to laugh; of course, she would say something like that. But Kay just leaned out the window and waved, her white hair streaking the blue curtains.

"See you later. I wasn't cooking dinner anyway," she called, half proudly, as if to say she had better things to do, and half sadly, it seemed to Dean, since there were no more youngsters to cook for. At 18, Zoe Mae was the youngest, and despite her spoiled-child, only-girl status, she was the most independent of all the children. The kids agreed that Paul was really the baby of the family.

Dean's Jeep gleamed red like the plastic bobbers he used for fishing. Every Sunday before Zoe Mae had hit adolescence, he had taken her down to the Bouquet by the skeletal remains of a turn-of-the-century inn where the fishing was best, and rigged her up with one of his old rods, as Vernon had done with him. They would spend the entire afternoon in tranquil silence, no other brothers allowed.

"Want to drive?"

She looked at him suspiciously for he never let anyone behind the wheel of his precious vehicle. She'd begged him for years, but he'd always refused.

"Why're you being so nice to me all of a sudden?" She walked to the passenger side. "No thanks. I don't trust you today."

"Suit yourself."

York Ferry's few lights glimmered behind them in the dusk as they headed east to Lakeshore Drive. It was June, and the summer people were just arriving for the season. They drove sleek new cars that bottomed out on the dirt mountain roads, threw loud parties on their decks keeping the whole town awake some nights, and raced their motorboats across the lake at three in the morning. The summer before, a sixteen-year-old girl drowned when she tried to water-ski at dawn, drunk and stoned after an all-night party at her parents' boathouse. From the state liquor store, the city people ordered cases of gin and vodka, and if they bumped into locals in the parking lot, they were always polite as they carefully maneuvered out of their way. But they held themselves aloof from York Ferry people, even when they drank at the inn or at Champlain's, and their closest connection to the people who lived here year-round was to hire them, usually to clean and serve.

"Shit, look at that place," Zoe Mae said, pointing to a house that had three new-looking cars in front, a sailboat and motorboat in back, and at least five bedrooms, although there were only two kids in the family. She leaned over and banged the horn twice, then propped her legs on the dash, her long red braid hanging out the window and thumping against the side of the Jeep.

"I don't love these people either, Zoe Mae, but at least they bring some money into town. York Ferry would be in even worse shape without them." He looked for her response, but she remained unconvinced. "Steve and the twins have made some serious money working down here, right?" She didn't affirm or deny it. "Still, I'm glad I don't have to depend on them to pay bills." While Dean didn't hate the summer people the way Zoe

Mae did, he preferred to have as little contact with them as possible.

"Amen, brother Dean. That's why I'm getting out of here. No money, no jobs, no nothing."

"Is that so?" He tried not to raise his voice. "You call four brothers, a sister-in-law, a niece, a nephew, and a mother, not to mention a shitload of friends, nothing?"

"Oh, I didn't mean it like that." She sighed. "I'm not going away forever. I just want to do something different. I don't want to check groceries my whole life at the IGA like Mom, or be some secretary in a stupid office like most of the girls in my class. None of them can even imagine leaving town. They wouldn't even move to P-burgh!"

"I sure can't see you all spiffed up behind a desk, Zoe Mae. You don't even wear dresses." He laughed, his broad face breaking into delicate lines by his eyes.

"It's out of the question, right? And what other choices do I have? I'm not a good enough mechanic to follow in our famous father's footsteps and rescue the reputation of the York Ferry Garage, although I did consider it, and I sure as hell don't want to clean bathtubs for these lazy asses out here, take out their garbage and entertain their boring kids."

He watched her scowling out the window and wished he could change things; it was harder for her than for the boys, although he wasn't exactly sure why. "I know there's not much for you to do here. I just don't like the idea of you signing your life away to something totally untried. You have no idea if you'll like being at sea, or living so far from home. What if you hate it? What if you're sick all the time? What then?"

Dean pulled the Jeep off the pavement at Elbow Beach, where the road angled left and the strip of land narrowed to a point, curving like a gull's wing to form one of York Ferry's swimming bays. No one else was there; the night had turned cool, and the other side of the lake sparkled with the sparse light of Vermont's scattered towns. The water lapped the shore in a steady, soothing rhythm; bullfrogs and crickets added their occasional noises. "You'll miss this," he said, shutting off the ignition and then starting for the tip of the sandy peninsula. He heard her calling for him to wait while she took off her boots and rolled up her jeans. She was twelve inches shorter than Dean, and he was halfway down the point before she caught up.

"Don't you think I know that?" she said, splashing in the water up to her knees, soaking the cuffs of her jeans, wincing at the cold but not complaining.

Dean felt defeated; his sister wasn't afraid of anything. How could he explain that sometimes fear was the right response, that even he would be frightened to give control of his life to the service, to take him away from home for so long?

"Aren't you too short, anyway? Don't they have height minimums for sailors?" He looked down at her sloshing noisily beside him, the back of her neck near her braid a pale patch of skin gleaming dully in the moonlight. That part of her body must never have seen the sun because it had no freckles. He remembered the day Zoe Mae was born and panicked at the thought that she wouldn't always be there.

"They used to. I'm part of the new anti-discrimination era, the lady on the phone said. They have to take me as long as I'm healthy, which I definitely am, having avoided the perils of drink that Paul so considerately illustrates for me daily." She took Dean's hand; her own was small but strong, unwavering. "I know you're supposed to try and change my mind. Mom's all upset about it, but can't you just understand? I know you do, Dean."

At that moment, he wished his father were there to tell her No. No, she couldn't go; he wouldn't permit it. Because Zoe Mae was only three when Vernon left, Dean was the closest thing she had to a father. Kay had always treated him like an adult after the disappearance. Together, he and his mother supported the rest of them. Zoe Mae was Kay's favorite, and his favorite, and he didn't want her to leave them alone.

"Have you thought about the things that might happen out

there?" He gestured eastward. "Besides all the technical stuff on a boat that could go wrong, like sinking, or catching on fire, you might get picked on 'cause you're so little, and you wouldn't have four brothers to threaten them with, or go beat them up for you like you do here."

She laughed. "You never did that anyway."

"Still, it was always a possibility. And what about a shipful of guys—'cause there can't be too many girls as crazy as you to be out there—who get a little cabin fever after a few months at sea? Do you get what I'm saying? The guys are going to be all over you, Zoe Mae, all the time. And there won't be a place to escape to."

"I'm not worried about that." Zoe Mae snorted. "If you're trying to scare me, you're not succeeding. You just don't want me to leave because," she paused, looking down at the water as if the appropriate words might be floating there, and she could just skim the surface to pick them up, "because of your own problems with it. You and Mom and all my friends, you're trying to talk me out of it because it makes *you* feel bad. It's got nothing to do with me." She stopped walking and let go of his hand.

"That's not true," Dean said, realizing it was at least partially true. He shut his eyes and tried to get all emotion out of his voice. "Think you're pretty damn important, don't you, Pumpkin-head?"

She didn't laugh.

"It's true, isn't it? I thought you were all so worried about my well-being or something. Jesus. I had it all wrong." She turned around and started for the Jeep, but Dean grabbed her braid and held it in his fist.

"Ouch! Let go."

He held on tight; she didn't move. They stood motionless for what seemed a very long time. He pretended Zoe Mae's hair was a fishing line, and he could just reel her back in if he wanted to, reel her in and put her in a bucket so she couldn't get away.

She was breathing calmly, slowly, not resisting at all. The black

108

ridges of the Adirondacks were silhouetted against the night, and the early constellations were already visible. The waves rippled, and a fish splashed suddenly.

"Of course I'll miss you," she said.

He hung on. As long as he had her braid in his hand, she couldn't grow up and go away, deserting them as they had been left behind before, a band of orphans.

But they couldn't stand there forever.

"I know you will, Zoe Mae. I'm sure of it." He let her go.

When she told him she wanted to walk home, he didn't try to argue. He backed out to the road and flashed his brights: she looked so young, carrying her boots, waving with her free hand.

Chapter Nine

1976

Exhausted, Kay collapsed on the porch, surveying the Pinny homestead: spring was budding on the row of maples that divided their land from the Bakers', infusing the air with the scent and smell of summer to come, and of autumn not far behind. She hated admitting she felt too tired to work the garden this year. The far fields, across the Short Bay Road, looked good for early grazing; she hoped she could rent them again to that hippie couple who kept sheep and spun their own wool. York Ferry people thought it scandalous that the unmarried couple lived with their baby in a converted yellow schoolbus on rented land, but Kay couldn't see much difference between that and trailers, which were standard North Country dwellings. Tucked behind the railroad-tie fence sat the wide plot for her vegetable garden, beside it the smaller one for flowers, which were admired in midsummer by the people in town. She grew a jungle of zinnias, phlox, gladioli, and always an experimental flower—last year she'd tried nasturtium—but the cars that slowed and stopped to gaze had made the trip to see Kay's sunflowers.

Kay loved sunflowers more than any other flower. It was a lucky coincidence they produced the seeds adored by her children and grandchildren. If she didn't do the vegetables this year, Kay decided, she would at least plant sunflowers. Kay recalled the story she used to read to Zoe Mae about the little girl, Clytie, who would daydream all afternoon instead of listening to her mother. One day, Apollo, driving his chariot across the sky, looked down to find the girl staring up at him, transfixed, while her mother called and called. Day after day, Clytie ignored her mother, gazing instead at the sun god when she should have been doing her chores. In punishment, Apollo melded her big brown eyes into one huge eye which filled her face, and her blonde hair stiffened into yellow petals, her body fusing into an upright green stalk. And that's why the sunflower turns its head toward the sun, following its path across the sky from morning till dusk, she would tell Zoe Mae, who would beg her mother to read it again. Ever since discovering that story, Kay liked to think of sunflowers as animated beings, blonde versions of her own redheaded Zoe Mae, bright and bold girl-children who defied the rules. As a child, Kay had sought to defy her mother at every turn. Now she felt lonely without Eleanor to rebel against.

The soil in both plots, to Kay's dismay, resembled granite and would need a powerful tilling, something she had always done herself since Vernon went away. First with just a spade, as he had done it, then with a borrowed rototiller, and finally, she'd bought her own. But even the machine required an enormous amount of energy. And then the weeding, gopher traps, ant patrol, canning, freezing… She couldn't bear to think about all that work, not to mention the endless, endless watering.

Kay sipped coffee from her favorite mug, yellow, with large brown polka dots, and propped her legs up on the peeling wooden rail. The whole porch needed painting, she noted. More work, and more money. Kay was 56 years old, and only Paul, of all her five children, remained at home with her. He was more often a burden than a help in her semi-old age, she thought, then immediately felt guilty. But there it was ten o'clock on a Saturday morning, and Paul hadn't yet arrived home from last night. He couldn't be more different from his twin, who worked diligently behind the IGA meat counter (her old job, from before she married) and who had just married a sensible girl from Port Elizabeth who was *not* pregnant on her wedding day. Paul, who remained penniless no matter how often he chose to work, thought all he had to do on this earth was have a good time. He drank, and he went home with any girl who'd invite him. Many did, since he was beautiful to look at, embarrassingly so to Kay, whose other children were solid, healthy people, not extraordinary looking. Paul and Joe shared a profile, a straight small nose and lush lips, so they had to be twins, although Kay had often wondered if the nurse at Plattsburgh General had somehow made a mistake in identifying Paul as her son. Joe was much more like her: steady, hardworking, disciplined. Strangers asked if Paul were Irish because he had the tongue of a storyteller, the love of drink, and the kind of smile that made women act foolish to get his attention.

Her other children reproached Kay for putting up with his behavior for the last few years, for actually encouraging it by not objecting loudly enough. But if he moved out, she'd be alone, and her nightmare of turning into a bent crone with a cane, stumbling around the house, prevented her from being harsher with him. And, despite his happy demeanor, Paul was the saddest child; Kay believed he had somehow been the most affected by Vernon's departure. Dean, too, had gotten into trouble at a younger age, getting Cathy pregnant just out of high school, but he had worked two jobs to feed his family and to help the rest of them. So he had little in common with Paul, who had gotten more than one girl pregnant, Kay knew, and had offered them nothing. One gave the baby up for adoption; the other had an abortion. Paul had nothing to do with either of them now.

There he was, walking down the road, hobbling really, unsteady on his feet from last night's alcohol. What a wreck he was at twenty-one! He wouldn't live much longer if he kept on like this, Kay had told him again and again, but he didn't listen, or didn't care. Paul had no concept of self-preservation, and she wondered if she had failed him, her youngest boy, in some terrible way that she could not identify. The rest of them were careful people, including Vernon before his disappearance.

"Good morning, Mother," Paul called from the driveway, his voice cheery and strained. "What do you think of my latest vehicle? Picture this: a cherry red GTO fresh off the line from Detroit. Black leather interior, chrome shining like the sun, the sweetest sound system on four wheels anywhere. Like it?" He gestured toward an imaginary car, pointing out its various features as if he were a game show host describing the grand prize. It was a ritual with them, a perverse exercise Paul invented after totaling the only car he'd ever owned, and then his best friend's. The state took his license away after the last accident, in which he rolled Kenny Heller's Chevy down a hill into the lake, walking away from it with a scratch on his left cheek that hadn't even left a scar. Paul managed to talk his way out of a jail term for driving under the influence. Kay almost wished he'd had to spend some time locked up; perhaps it would have made a difference. If there was a god, and Kay sorely doubted it, then He was spending His time looking after her youngest boy. He had luck, her Paul, but for how much longer? Something would break in him; she worried about Paul constantly.

"Doesn't look like such a good morning to me, Paul Vernon. Your eyes are bloodshot, your clothes look filthy, and you don't smell very good. I can tell from way over here."

"You know flattery gets you everywhere with me. Once I take a shower I'll be better than ever." He lurched onto the porch and kissed her forehead. "You, on the other hand, smell like sweetest spring, Kayleen."

She pushed him away, trying to be stern, but he had melted her anger, as he always did. "Go clean up and get to bed, please. When you're a human being again, let me know."

"Yes, Ma'am." Paul saluted and clicked his heels before going inside, where she heard the telltale sound of a beer bottle opening, the smack of lips, the engorging of Paul's gullet, then the bottle falling into the trash.

Sighing, Kay fished a cigarette out of the bib pocket of

Vernon's overalls, the well-patched pair she always wore for garden work. Swallowing another sip of coffee, she grimaced, then threw the dregs over the rail, wanting more but too tired to get up. Another week ripped from the calendar. Cashiering full-time at the IGA was getting to be too much for her; the very marrow of her bones ached. And she could afford to work less, now that her expenses were reduced to feeding only herself and Paul, paying the power company and the telephone. And the food was discounted, of course. Fortunately, Vernon had paid off the mortgage before he left, working twelve-hour days, six days a week. How long had he planned his departure? Since their wedding? Now Zoe Mae was out on a Coast Guard cruiser somewhere, and Steve was independent, living alone at the camp in Port Elizabeth. Dean and Joe were solvent, even saving money for the future. Kay again surveyed the hard ground. Any of her sons would volunteer to till the garden if she let them know she needed help, but it was such a hard thing to admit.

"Telephone!" Paul was calling. "It's for you."

She hadn't heard it ring, but lately she imagined her hearing was faltering. She trudged to the kitchen.

"Hello, is this Kay?"

"Yes?"

"It's Averill. Averill Forster. From work. How are you?"

"Just fine. I'm getting ready to start the garden this year."

"That's an awful lot of work, Kay. Is your son helping you?"

She looked over at Paul, who was surveying the contents of the refrigerator, the alcoholic smell of his clothing wafting over to where she stood. "Well, no. I haven't asked him to. You see, I really take pleasure in doing the tilling myself." There. She would have to do it now.

"If you change your mind, let me know. I couldn't offer my help, of course, because of my back. But I have a big, strong 25-year-old son just lazing around here with nothing to do who owes me a favor or two, and he'd get your place tilled in no time at all."

114

"Thanks for the offer, Averill, but I don't think so."

"Kay? I, aah, I was wondering if you'd like to drive up to Plattsburgh with me this evening and maybe go to a nice seafood restaurant, and perhaps take in a show later."

A date. He was asking her on a date, and she hadn't been on one in thirty years, not since Vernon asked her to go for a drive that chill afternoon when he'd finished repairing the clutch on her old Ford, back in her butcher days, when she and the IGA were young and attractive.

"When?"

"Tonight, if you'd like. Or some other time, if you'd prefer." Averill Forster was fifteen years her senior, a widower for nearly the same length of time that Kay had been alone. (She'd never been able to come up with a good, accurate term for her wifely status, refusing to call herself "deserted" or "abandoned," and she'd never pursued a divorce, seeing no particular reason to drag her life into a courtroom.)

"I guess I'm not doing anything special tonight. That sounds like a nice change of routine. But do they have seafood in P-burgh?"

"My son-in-law works at The Captain's Table. He says it's the best food in town."

"All right, then. Shall I meet you there?"

"Oh, no! I'll pick you up. Say, 6:30?"

"Fine. I'll see you then, then."

Replacing the receiver, she shivered, half-elated, half-petrified. A date. Vernon would laugh. He'd say Averill Forster was too old for her. They used to call him a fuddy-duddy back in the forties when they thought he had eyes for Kay, before he married.

"Who was that?" Paul reappeared in the kitchen wearing only a towel wrapped around his waist, cleaning his ear with a Q-tip. He looked a hundred times better now, his body in surprisingly good shape from the occasional handyman jobs he found on the lakeshore. The alcohol hadn't yet put a bulge in his belly.

"Do I ask *you* who called every time the phone rings?"

"Pardon me, Madam. I just thought it sounded as if you had a date this evening."

"I do," she said in a small voice. She hadn't even considered what Paul might think.

"With who?" He sounded more curious than upset.

"Averill Forster."

"Your boss?"

"Is something wrong with that?"

"Mother, it's bad form to go out with people from work, and most especially your boss."

"Oh? What would you know about that? Work, I mean."

"Feeling a little snappy this morning, aren't we? I'm the one with the hangover."

"Don't remind me."

"I work. When's the last time I asked you for money?"

She thought for a moment. "Last month."

"But that was only a loan. I'll pay you back. Next week. This odd-job thing is working out pretty well. I buy my own clothes and tools, my music, my own booze. Gas for my car."

Kay turned away to hide her grin. "Well, but you've—what shall we say—spent your free time with some of those young ladies from the Lakeshore Drive." Paul had crossed one of the invisible boundaries separating the summer people from the locals by flagrantly courting the daughters of some of the wealthier families.

"That's completely different. You have a regular job, nine to five, every day. I just skip around. What if, for example, Forster did something tonight that made you uncomfortable? Nothing sinister. Just say it didn't go so well, say you felt awkward all evening. Would you then feel funny at the supermarket around him? Would you have to consider quitting your job? There's a lot of little details to consider here."

She looked him over, wincing. "Oh, this is great, isn't it? My twenty-one-year-old hungover son comes home on a Saturday morning to give his mother advice on dating. That's just lovely."

116

"Relax. Times are changing."

"They don't change that much. I feel silly."

"Why should you feel silly?"

Kay shrugged, then went to the stove to heat more coffee. "Want some?

"Mother, I would absolutely die for some."

"Paul, I swear I don't know where you came from. You're nothing like me, nor are you like Vernon."

"What about the milkman?"

"We never *had* a milkman, and I don't appreciate that kind of humor. You know I've never been with anyone but your father." As she said it, she pictured Vernon the morning he left, sixteen years ago. The man who never returned. She would die before she humbled herself by asking him to come back. He had walked out on her and the kids, and they didn't crumple and fall apart.

"But how come Zoe Mae's hair is so very, very red?"

"Your father had bright red hair as a child," Kay retorted, coloring.

"I know that." Paul accepted the steaming mug, smiling up at her gratefully. "I'm just giving you a hard time."

"Don't, please. I feel very odd about going on a date."

They sat together at the kitchen table, filling only two of the seven chairs.

"You wouldn't get married again, would you?" Paul's usually confident manner faltered momentarily. "I mean, not that you shouldn't."

"Sweetie, I barely talk to Averill beyond the price of peas. I'm not thinking about marriage, believe me."

"I'll bet he is, though. He'll ask you. Not tonight, but eventually. He's alone, you're alone, and I'll bet he's always had his eye on you. It's taken him a hell of a long time to get his courage up to ask you out. Must be a cautious kind of guy. You wouldn't worry he would up and do something impulsive on you."

"You're out of line here." She stared into her coffee, avoiding

Paul's comment on Vernon. "Besides, I'm not alone. You're here."

"I'll bet I'm right. Let's put this on the calendar and see how many weeks it takes him to propose. He'd love to have you cooking his dinner in that big empty house he has up there by the Northway."

"I'm not interested in moving anywhere, you can bet on that, nor am I planning to be anybody's housekeeper." She huffed. "Including yours, I should remind you."

Paul ignored the rebuke. "I didn't mean he doesn't like you, or that he's only trying to get you to clean house for him. I'm sure he cares for you." Paul spoke softly, looking out the window toward the fallow fields.

"Let's not talk about it, okay? Can you help me get the tiller going? Or are you too tired?"

"It's the weekend, Mom. Miller time. Time for me and my favorite gal, Jenny Cream."

"Forget it, then. I'll call Dean."

"No. I'll do it. I'll never hear the end of it if I don't." He drained his mug. "Let me throw on some jeans."

She watched him go, shaking her head, knowing that she would let him get away with almost anything.

After dragging the machine out from the shed, Paul gassed it and made sure nothing was amiss. He'd inherited his father's instinctive understanding of engines. It was noon by this time, and he was drinking another bottle of beer. She hated to reprimand him—it didn't do any good—but she hated saying nothing, which made her feel like a silent accomplice to his self-destruction. He placed the tiller on the edge of the vegetable plot and started it up. Earth churned, its rocky texture yielding to the blades. The roar was deafening.

"You sure you don't want me to do it?" he shouted.

"No. I like doing it. Go to bed."

Wearily, he walked back up the hill to the house, finishing his Jenny Cream in one long swallow.

118

Kay gripped the handles, trying to get accustomed to the vibrations. Had she really done this for fifteen years? Her arms looked so puny below the rolled-up flannel shirt, her wrists thin and old-ladyish. Maybe gloves would help. She shut down the machine and went searching in the shed for last year's pair.

The air smelled of Paul's sweat in here, of his body leaking alcohol. Even after he showered, his perspiration reeked of whiskey. The garden gloves hung on a hook off the pegboard, which was adorned with Vernon's wrenches and ratchets, carefully arranged in order of size. Paul had kept everything as it was. For Kay, the shed remained her husband's domain. Underneath the workbench, something colorful peeped out from a pile of rags. She uncovered a stack of *Penthouse* and *Playboy* magazines, obviously belonging to Paul since they were recent. Frowning, she opened one and leafed through it, disgusted. The poses were so unnatural, so phony. How could any man be deceived by the plastic smiles? Paul could have any young woman he went after, Kay thought, so why buy these expensive magazines? For all her son's womanizing, including the two girls he got into trouble, Paul had never really had a girlfriend. He said York Ferry girls were dull, and he hadn't met anyone yet he cared to spend time with. In his thirst for something different, he ran off to Plattsburgh to enlist for Vietnam, but when his medical exam showed arrhythmia of the heart, he was rejected. Paul didn't want some desk job in the States, so he dropped his application.

She would talk to him about this later, Kay decided, putting the magazines back exactly where she'd found them and pulling on the too-large cotton gloves. No, she was being ridiculous, imagining she could tell Paul what he could and couldn't read. She couldn't tell any of her children anything anymore, especially Zoe Mae, who had never listened to her anyway.

It was a good day for tilling, she admitted, taking in the clear blue sky. The house was up on a slight rise, its frame sagging to the east What was that called? Settling. The Pinny farmhouse was still settling after all this time. The shed, also sagging, though in the opposite direction, squatted at the end of the driveway, below the house by several yards, and the garden plots were below it. Vernon had planted them so the furrows were parallel to the slope of the hill; for irrigation they relied on gravity, leaving the hose at the top of the plot. And he'd dug drainage ditches out to the road so that the plants at the bottom wouldn't flood. Probably, after almost thirty years of harvesting in the same spot, she should move the gardens. She had nineteen acres, after all. But if she started anew in another part of the property, she wouldn't be able to remember Vernon in it, the way he'd carefully mapped out the area and engineered the drainage. She wouldn't be able to stand in the spot where they'd experimented with exotic plants like eggplant and artichokes, real pioneers, only to fall back, after failure, on standard North Country fare: carrots, corn, tomatoes. Averill Forster had never tilled a garden; she couldn't picture his frail torso or his pale hands browned by dirt or sun.

Back at the edge of the plot, she placed her boot securely on the footrest and hit the switch. Nothing happened. She flipped it on and off several times, but the machine was dead. Kay hated these contraptions although she'd certainly taken advantage of them during the last several years. The thought of tilling by spade was too exhausting to consider. She didn't want to wake Paul when he clearly needed his sleep, so she went back to her perch in the heavy Adirondack chair she kept on the porch in winter, and on the lawn in summer. It was warm enough today to bring it onto the grass. She pulled it toward the steps, its wooden feet making a horrible scraping noise against the floor. It barely moved; she'd forgotten how heavy it was. Such an awkward piece of furniture, with all its weight in the lowest part near the ground. If she couldn't move a chair twenty feet, she certainly wouldn't be able to run a tiller all afternoon.

Now she resolved to move the chair with no more nonsense and then till the garden, and she'd be done. Kay wrestled with the unwieldy green wood before it slipped from her grasp and tumbled down the six steps to the ground, bouncing hard on her left instep.

After it landed, she sat in the chair facing the wrong way, rocking her aching foot. What an awful day it was turning out to be. Instead of looking out to the lake and the mountains, the chair faced the house, and she could see every peeling plank, every hole and nick in the facade. If Vernon had stayed, he would have kept it up, painted it when it needed painting, patched the roof before it began to leak instead of after. She'd done her best, but maintaining a hundred-year-old farmhouse with five children tearing it apart while they grew had been no easy chore. Her foot stopped throbbing, finally, but still hurt. She got up and dragged the chair to its proper spot, with its wide view overlooking a good chunk of Madnan's Valley, including the upright, motionless tiller. Why not call Averill Forster and have his son do it? Nobody would need to know; Paul would sleep until dark, and she wouldn't have to admit to her children that she was no longer strong enough. Resolved, she made the call and then easily wheeled the broken tiller back to the shed. Simon Forster was bringing his own machine.

Without pausing a minute, he tilled both plots, his broad back sweating vigorously through an olive T-shirt, Vietnam dog tags hanging from a long chain around his neck. He barely acknowledged her presence, and initially declined the plate of bologna sandwiches and lemonade she brought when he had finished.

"Got any beer?"

Reluctantly, she got him a bottle from Paul's supply, which he drank in one long swallow, standing by his station wagon after loading the tiller.

"Would you like another?" She felt obligated to please him.

"Yeah. I'll try one of those sandwiches now, too."

She wondered if she should pay him something but decided to leave that question until later, when she would consult Averill.

Simon finished the sandwiches, drank a glass of lemonade

and got in his car. "What happened to your old man?"

Stunned by his bluntness, Kay stuttered, "He...He's not here."

"I know that much. I'm wondering what happened to him. He's been gone a long time now, isn't he?"

"Sixteen years ago June twelfth." She liked to make the details clear about Vernon's disappearance, as if knowing the exact details of how compensated for the blurry complexity of why. He'd left a trail of letters for Kay to follow, but she had declined his overtures. He'd chosen the memory of a girl over herself and their family, and she didn't forgive him that. No matter what was troubling Kay, she would never desert her own children, no matter who was there to care for them.

Simon was examining the dragon tattoos on his arms, ugly, eerily etched creatures writhing along his biceps, gunning the engine, apparently ignoring her, but still he didn't leave. "He fought in Europe, didn't he?"

"Yes. In the Air Force, as a mechanic. His unit helped save Bastogne from the Germans."

"I didn't save anyone from anything," Simon said. "I said burn that village, and it burned. I followed orders. Simon said shoot, and they shot. My boys always listened to their leader, just like the game. Whatever Simon said. I have a drawerful of ears. Sweet Jesus." He wiped his forehead and stared at his reflection in the rear-view mirror. "It's fucking hard to come back to this sleepy, stupid town where everything stays the same, only you're not the same as when you left, not anywhere near the same, after you've lived so long in hell. And then they expect you to act normal or something. Whatever the fuck that is. My father wants me to work at the goddamn supermarket, can you believe that?" He looked at Kay as if she would certainly share his contempt. But she said nothing, riveted by the fusillade of words. "My father wasn't in the war, that war they call the good war, because of his sorry-ass back. Not like your husband. So long, lady. Have a nice time tonight with old Dad." He floored the wagon and sped out of sight, leaving a faint curtain of dust over the Short Bay Road and a feeling of dread in Kay's stomach.

By 6 o'clock she didn't want to go anymore, but she was afraid to call and say she'd changed her mind. Simon had frightened her a little, but that wasn't the whole reason. Vernon was haunting the farmhouse, lingering in the smell of just-turned earth. She took a shower and put on her favorite spring dress, an indigo high-waisted jumper with a three-quarter-sleeved white dickey, and then took it off. Sitting in her slip on the edge of the bed, smoking, she wished Paul would get up so they could talk, but he wouldn't for a while yet unless she woke him, which she was reluctant to do.

Would Averill Forster try to touch her tonight? To kiss her? He was a kind man, and she admired him and the gentle but firm way he did business, but she'd never thought he was somebody to kiss. Even considering it made her queasy: his gray moustache would be hard and bristly and smell of cigars. Vernon, of course, was only thirty-seven years old in her memory, with a healthy young man's body and strong hands that knew how to hold her, securely and with passion, in this bed at night with the lights off. Most of the time, she still thought of herself as only forty, as having the same body and mind she had when Vernon walked out the door on that cool, green morning. But now, looking at her bony shoulders in the mirror, the lines feathering out from her eyes, her white cloud of hair, she knew she was not the same anymore. If Vernon walked in the door this minute, he wouldn't find the woman he'd left; that soft wife had been replaced by a hard old woman.

Someone was knocking at the front door, and she called out, "Who is it?" before looking at the clock. "Let yourself in, Averill. I'll be right there."

By the time she'd put the dress back on, applied lipstick and wiped it off, tried on some dressy heels that made her feet hurt and were at least five years out of fashion, Kay hoped Averill Forster had changed his mind. But she spied his small body seated primly on the couch; Paul was walking around the room with a beer in hand, half-dressed, telling him stories, or outright lies, about the parties on the lakeshore.

"I'm sorry I kept you waiting."

"Oh, that's all right. Paul here was looking after me."

"So, Mrs. Vernon Pinny, I hear you had Simon over here this afternoon to till the garden."

"Why, yes. You were sleeping all afternoon, remember?"

"I told you I would do it!" He tried to control his anger, which had evidently been building since he'd learned about Simon.

"I didn't want to wake you. The tiller broke."

"I would have fixed it! You know I would have fixed it."

"Kay? I think we should get a move on if we want to catch that movie later."

"Yeah, you better go. I wouldn't want to keep you," said Paul as he tossed the empty bottle halfway across the room into a garbage basket. Averill Forster watched open-mouthed.

As Kay put on her coat and stepped out to the porch in front of his outstretched arm, he said, "You look very nice tonight."

After she thanked him, Kay heard Paul mimicking Averill Forster's compliment like a parrot, and then a falsetto, "Thank you, Averill."

"I guess Paul's a little upset with me." She laughed uneasily as he backed his Chrysler down the driveway while every light in the house lit up, and the stereo blasted raucous rock-and-roll. Kay cringed.

"Looks like he's having a party tonight," he said.

"Probably by himself." Kay hated to think that Paul blamed her for betraying him somehow, for betraying Vernon, too, when all she was doing was growing old. She gritted her teeth and attempted a smile, determined to enjoy herself in spite of her son, despite her own murky feelings about Averill Forster and what it meant to finally pay attention to another man.

"So what are you planting in your garden this year?" he asked politely, turning onto the Short Bay Road, headed north for Plattsburgh. Kay felt as if she were leaving home forever.

"Same stuff as always, I guess: corn, squash, beans, lettuce, carrots. Sunflowers." She looked in the side mirror and saw the house disappear behind her. "No, maybe not sunflowers."

She was finished with sunflowers. And next year she would move the garden to where the soil wasn't so exhausted.

Chapter Ten

1977

A leaf escaped from the coverlet as Cathy made the bed, drifting leisurely to the floor as if falling from a dying oak. Between the sheets she found another: new maple, heartbreakingly green and intact. Tonight, she decided, she would ask Dean—no, tell Dean—to leave this house. Cathy had returned from a weekend in Glens Falls with the kids to find sand and grass and the smell of the woods in their bedroom. Dean had slept with someone else in her private domain, infecting the very air with deceit. Whoever it was liked to roll around in the dirt with him; she didn't. Dean was at work, the kids in school, her sisters unavailable, so she had no one to tell. Sitting in her mother's rocking chair, she clutched the smooth cotton sheets she'd intended to wash, since it was Monday, but now decided to save, if necessary, for evidence.

Later, in the car, driving over the Bouquet River Bridge, she didn't know what to do. When the IGA Supermarket appeared, she made a sudden left into the parking lot; she could use a few things at the house. Both her mother-in-law and brother-in-law worked there, but she hoped neither would be around. The quiet twin, Joe, had always been moony around her, and once Dean said straight out that his little brother was in love with her. They'd both laughed about it. Poor Joe, short and chubby and plain, was still afflicted at twenty-two with severe acne. Cathy cringed to think of his adolescence, how he'd suffered the most from the Pinny legacy. He was nothing like Dean, who was always popular (she smiled ruefully), nor an athlete like Steve, who'd been taunted for his quietness but was still respected as a track star. And Joe wasn't at all like his twin, who was boisterous and drank and breezed through school on the grace of his extravagant smile. Although Joe was married now, his wife pregnant, Cathy still felt funny around him, aware of her disquieting effect.

Fortunately, he wasn't in. But Kay was, checking out customers in the only cashier lane open. Her mother-in-law, unlike her sons, had never been overly fond of her. Cathy put her milk, eggs, and Rice Krispies on the black rubber counter. When Kay hit the foot-toggle, the revolving belt, moaning and humming, carried the items toward her as if on a stubborn, muddy tide.

"Hello there." Kay smiled, as she would at any customer, Cathy thought. "Are you all right?" Her voice rose with concern. "You look awfully pale."

"I'm fine," Cathy said, but then she didn't feel so fine. Her legs wobbled, and she tried to remember if she'd eaten anything that day. Had she only drunk coffee? She swayed.

"Sit down here," Kay ordered, then steered her daughter-in-law around the stacks of brown bags to the chair she kept behind the register; there were long slack periods at the IGA since they'd built the super-sized Grand Union in Plattsburgh. "Let me get you a glass of water." She scurried off to the cooler.

Cathy fished a compact from her pocketbook; she did look peaked, with deep circles sunk in the hollows above her cheekbones. Even her hair looked tired, sitting limply on her shoulders, its rich blonde faded to a milky colorlessness. Before Kay returned she snapped the mirror shut; her mother-in-law thought she was vain, which bothered Cathy.

"Maybe," Kay said thoughtfully, looking Cathy up and down as if she were a sack of potatoes on sale and she was trying to find the price sticker, "maybe you and Dean need a vacation. Why not let the kids stay with me for a while? Or just stay home and get Dean to take a day off, and loll around the house?"

Cathy looked at her lap, hands folded solemnly.

Kay spoke less confidently. "Or maybe you need some time to yourself. Give me the kids and take off for a couple of days."

"I just got back from Glens Falls, Kay. Just this morning."

"But you had the kids with you, right? That's not really a vacation."

"Kay, you've never taken a vacation in your life," Cathy said, smiling. "The kids aren't the problem, anyway." She sipped icy water from the Styrofoam cup, and, feeling stronger, looked her mother-in-law in the eye. She didn't know how much was safe to say, how much allegiance Kay had toward her son, how much she valued Cathy as the mother of her grandchildren, and how much she might commiserate as the wife of a difficult man.

"What *is* the problem, then?" Kay sounded more curious than hostile, but still Cathy wondered if she could trust her with the truth. Just then, old Mr. Morissey, owner of the Champlain Bar & Grill, George Reiser's competition, brought up his purchases to be checked out. He had six boxes of macaroni and cheese, a loaf of bread, a package of bacon, and a pound of ground beef. "Charlie, shouldn't you get some vegetables, too?" Kay asked as she accepted his money and counted out the change. Cathy put his things into a doubled paper bag.

"Mind your own business, why don't you?" he said to Kay, then, "Thank you, young lady," to Cathy. He left, and the store was empty.

"Always a sweetheart, that old man," Kay said. "Thanks for helping. You didn't need to do that."

"It's no big deal." Cathy sat back down.

"You still haven't told me why you look so poorly today." Kay twirled a strand of white hair around her forefinger. "But I have a feeling I know."

Cathy sighed. "You know about Dean's girlfriend, then. Or girlfriends, I should say." She hated that word; it sounded so juvenile, like high school. Thirty-year-old married men with chil-

128

dren were not supposed to have girlfriends in their vocabulary.

"Dean's never told me about them, of course. But I've heard the stories in town, probably the same ones you have."

Cathy accepted Kay's offer of a Pall Mall and her plastic lighter. "What do you think I should do? What would you do if you were me?" She wondered if she'd get an honest answer.

"That's a pretty sticky question." Kay squeezed her eyes shut, furrowing her brow. "If I pretend I'm not involved in this, as if I didn't have a son and two grandchildren to consider, I'd say, hmmm. I'd walk out, I think. I'd take the kids and say good-bye." She opened her eyes. "But first, I'd try to find out why he needed to go to some other woman instead of his wife. Vernon and I had our problems, evidently, but infidelity wasn't on the list. Not exactly."

"I'm surprised you're not blaming me." Cathy exhaled a long, acrid column of smoke. "I mean, I thought you'd defend Dean to the end."

"Of course I'd defend Dean to the end." Kay smiled and picked a piece of tobacco off her teeth with a fingernail. "That's a whole different question. But if I were you, that's what I'd do. What I think I'd do, anyway. There are some things one mustn't put up with, Cathy. You need your dignity. Always."

The bells on the door tinkled, and a crowd of children appeared, shepherded by a man in his fifties with a John Deere cap. The children's hair was unkempt, their clothes mismatched and dirty.

"The Smithfields," Kay murmured, frowning. Everyone knew the oldest girl had a child by her father after the mother passed away. The baby had the same stricken eyes as the old man, who held him roughly under his arm.

"What are you going to do?" Kay asked.

"It's been going on for a while, you know, and I've put up with it because...I don't know exactly why. Because I couldn't imagine any other life than the one I've got. I've always been married to Dean. My whole adult life. And I couldn't separate him from the kids; he does love them.

"But this morning, when I found the dirt in the bed from one of his—what would you call them? outdoor excursions?—that was the last straw. He's rubbing my face in it. It's too much already. And with Dean contributing money for the kids, I can make a living. Other people make do." She considered her mother-in-law. "You do."

Kay looked at her intently, the pupils in her eyes expanded wide, like a cat's in a dim room. "How do you know he didn't just sleep outside by himself, if you don't mind my asking?"

"I guess I don't know for certain. But that's what happened the very first time with that Jewish girl, or whatever she was. It took me a while to figure it all out—those trips with the guys from work, his long nights at the Champlain. But Dean's no professional drinker, and I discovered that he doesn't like to play cards, even though he's apparently spent a lot of time at it." She sighed. "He finds these young girls who think he's so, I don't know, romantic. The romantic truckdriver with the heart of gold, just like those guys in the truckdriving songs he likes to listen to. You ever heard them?"

Kay nodded. "He's always liked them, even when he was a child."

"'Big Joe and Phantom 309'—that's his favorite. I think that's how Dean sees himself: as a guy who'd jackknife his truck and die for a schoolbus full of kids. Isn't that ridiculous?" She wanted to cry. "And he probably would, too. But would he do it for me?"

Kay patted her shoulder, which felt odd to Cathy, since the two women had almost never touched and rarely confided in one another since Dean and Cathy were married, twelve years before.

"Some things you're better off not thinking about." Kay handed her a tissue. "Because there's no rational answer in hell. Believe me. You need to make some plans. Actual things you can accomplish. I suppose you could work at the inn with your sister and father, huh?"

Cathy made a sour face. "Last resort only. I hate that place."

"So what are your choices, then?"

"Summer work. Like Steve or my sister Virginia. Do the season and get unemployment the rest of the year. I was thinking about hiring myself out as a cook on the Lakeshore Drive." Cathy thought it more and more possible.

"Don't they usually bring in their people from the city for that?"

"Not always. I know a girl from my class who was a housekeeper one summer for a family from Albany, government people. They liked her so much they took her back with them in September."

"Now, you're not planning on going away, are you?" Kay's voice hardened.

"No. Don't worry."

"All right, then." Her voice returned to normal. "For my own selfish reasons, I don't want you leaving York Ferry with the kids."

"Right now I haven't even talked to Dean, so I don't know what's going to happen. I better go. Dean, Jr., will be home from school soon." She stood up and smiled tentatively at Kay. "Thanks for listening."

"Call me later, Cathy. Let me know what happens." Then Kay walked calmly toward the back of the store where one of the Smithfield clan had overturned what sounded like an entire case of soda bottles.

At exactly 8 p.m., Dean's Jeep slowed and turned into the driveway. Cathy was practicing her speech, pacing the living room, when she heard him shut the car door, then crush the gravel as he plodded toward the back entrance. The kids were in bed but not yet asleep, their high-pitched laughter drifting down the stairs. She watched him come into the kitchen, hang his jeans jacket on the rack, remove his boots, cap, and run a dirty hand, twice, through his thick dark hair. He was so methodical;

131

the way he took off his clothes or put them on or did anything he did regularly was always in the same exact order without a hair's worth of variation. It comforted and maddened Cathy at the same time.

"I'm in here," she called from the couch, another Lakeshore Drive salvage with gold brocade upholstery. Dean switched on the lamp and looked down at her quizzically.

"You all right?"

"Just fine," she said deliberately. "You?"

"I'm beat," he said, stretching out beside her, his head hanging over the back of the sofa, his broad nose pointing up at the ceiling. A shadowy triangle of stubble remained beneath his left nostril where he'd missed shaving. She noticed a hole in the knee of his jeans and thought about patching it before it grew any bigger.

"Why so tired? I thought Mondays were easy."

"Not today, boy. The boss just rode my crew like a goddamn work horse. You know, the season's almost here"—he said *season* as if it were some kind of plague—"and they got us retarring the Lakeshore Drive now. So nobody gets a flat on their new Cadillac or something. Pisses me off."

"You said they were retarring a number of roads in the county, not just the Lakeshore."

"Pardon me. I didn't mean to insult your friends."

"They're not my friends. I don't even know anyone down there anymore." She glared at him. Damn it. This wasn't how she'd planned to begin their discussion. "You hungry?"

"Starving." Dean stood up and brushed his hands on the thighs of his jeans. She noted again how he'd never worn a wedding band, claiming that any jewelry was dangerous on the job. But she knew that his co-workers wore theirs.

"Kids still up? I'll say hi to them first and wash up."

In the kitchen, she arranged a plate of hamburger, peas, carrots and french fries. Everything was limp from sitting in the oven for the last two hours. Tough. She poured a glass of milk

132

and sat down in the chair opposite his to wait.

"Dean, we need to talk," she said calmly after he'd begun eating. He was so intent on getting food to his stomach that he failed to notice her seriousness.

"What? You need some more money or something?"

"No. I want you to leave. I want a divorce." It was a powerful word; he stopped eating.

"Did I hear you right?"

"A divorce," she repeated. "Immediately."

"Hold on a minute. What brought this on?"

Her lips tightened. "So you're going to play innocent, huh?"

"I don't know what you're talking about."

"I see." She folded her arms across her chest. A long silence followed, during which Dean resumed eating, though quite slowly, as he directed his attention to spearing peas onto the tines of his fork.

"I don't know what you're talking about."

"Oh, please," Cathy said, disgusted. "Can't you do better than that?"

"Cath, I'm tired. I've had a really hard day, and I'm not in the mood to play games with you." He pushed his plate away, unfinished, to a dangerous position half-off and half-on the table. Standing up, he drained the last of his milk. "When you want to talk to me instead of dancing around with this I-know-something-you-don't-know crap, then I'll talk. Otherwise, I'm going to bed."

"Had a hard night too, I guess. Saturday, maybe Sunday night as well. Remember? When your family was away." Cathy smiled, her mouth tightening into two thin-lipped lines. "You must remember, Dean, when you slept outside with your friend and then brought her here? Or maybe you didn't bring her here. Whatever you did, you left a lot of shit in our bed."

Dean sat down. "Wait a minute. I sleep outside when you're away, and you automatically assume I was with someone? That's ridiculous."

"You haven't denied it," she said, pushing the plate to safety.

"I'm denying it. Saturday night I slept on Madnan's Ridge, *by myself*, after fishing up at Little Falls all day. Steve didn't want to come, so I went alone. Ask him yourself." Dean seemed self-righteously proud of his explanation. For a minute, Cathy wondered if she'd made an enormous mistake.

"I will, then. Think back on another time, oh, say, three years ago, when we had a similar conversation about why there was sand in our bed? You said you'd been camping alone, and of course I believed you. I still trusted you then." She and Dean both reached for the pack of cigarettes by the salt shaker. He let her take one first; each used their own lighters.

"But you know how things are in this town. Sooner or later, everyone hears everything. Fred Reber told someone he saw you real early that Sunday morning, real early, with a girl in your Jeep with long black hair in a red dress. Or maybe her hair wasn't so long. You know how things get exaggerated."

Dean wiped his mouth with his hand and blew into his palm as if he were cold. "I don't see what that has to do with this weekend."

"But you're not denying that one, are you?" It was not a question, and she didn't wait for a response. "What about that tall redhead with braids down to her ass who worked with you on the road crew for a few weeks last summer? What about her? I hear she was studying engineering up at SUNY, or was it a crash course in truckdrivers?"

Dean's gaze was circling around the room, from floor to ceiling and back, avoiding Cathy completely.

"Pretty good information on my part, wouldn't you say? Your boss's wife and I sometimes go up to the mall together, and her husband tells her everything, just like you and me."

"Jesus, Cathy!" He finally looked at her, the blue in his eyes turned nearly black. "I thought you didn't care! Why didn't you ever say anything? Three years later you decide to confront me with a divorce—no discussion, no working it out? That's a great way of doing things."

"Oh. How would you do it?" She smiled icily. "I mean, say I'd been fooling around on you for three years? What would you do?"

He shifted and shifted in his chair, failing to find a comfortable position. "But you haven't. I mean, you're not." His tone was not confident.

"No, I haven't. Not that I've lacked for opportunities. Even your own dear work buddies at those drunken Christmas parties. And your boss, too, at the Fourth of July barbeque last year was awfully friendly to me, way beyond the call of duty. I guess he felt sorry for me."

"Really? Why didn't you tell me?"

"I didn't think you'd care, frankly."

Dean stood up, scratching at his mass of graying hair, and began to walk around the room, his large hands clasped behind his neck.

"Cathy, how can you say that? Of course I care. I had no idea about these guys. Who besides Joe White? What a pig he is!"

"So that's what's important to you. That your buddies are going behind your back. That your honor's been violated, or some other bullshit. Not that you and I might have a problem. If you do care about me, Dean, you sure show it in mysterious ways." It was difficult to gauge Dean's reaction because he kept moving, head tucked down behind the shield of his bent arms. "Like your father," she added. "Your father showed his devotion to his family in pretty bizarre ways too. Must run in the family, although I wish I'd figured that out earlier."

"Leave Vernon out of this. He's got nothing to do with you and me."

She didn't answer, unconvinced.

"Cathy, I don't know what to say. I won't do it anymore, okay? I promise. I'm sorry. I really thought it wouldn't matter to you."

"How could it not matter to me?" She wanted to scream.

"But we're always fighting, Cathy, always at each other."

"So? All couples fight. You can't have marriage without disagreements, for god's sake. We don't fight more than anybody else we know. What did you expect? That we would be eighteen years old forever, having the time of our lives every day?"

"No. I didn't think that." He stopped behind her chair, and she swiveled around to face him.

"What did you expect, then?"

"I just thought you'd be more like you were when we got married in the first place. When we had such a great time together, and you liked sleeping with me." Dean frowned. "You've changed so much during the last couple of years. All you want to do is mind the kids. It's like I'm not here."

Cathy was silent. Was he right? She did devote herself to the children; she wanted to. "Wait a second. The last couple of years are when you started sleeping around. So my relationship with the kids is what it is *because* of what you've done. I didn't provoke anything."

"No. That's not right. You'd changed before I ever did anything. And don't make it sound like I've slept with all these women. There's only been a couple."

"There've been a few more than a couple, Dean. Don't lie."

"Okay. A few more. But not so many. I don't do it all the time. A lot of guys at work do it all the time, some of those married guys on the crew who wear their wedding bands religiously."

Cathy paused. This wasn't going at all the way she'd planned. His answers were too easy, too pat.

"Some girls want you more if you're married, practically. The ring proves you're desirable, worth their chase. I've never pretended that I wasn't married. I'm not saying that as an excuse, though." He crouched on the floor, gripping her chair for balance, below her like a little boy. "For the last few years, I've felt that you don't really want me around. You'd rather be with the kids without me interfering. That's the impression I get. So what am I supposed to do?

"I really tried, in the beginning, to make all this effort to be home more and be more patient and all that, but I still got the feeling you were happier when I wasn't here. I got lonely." He pursed his lips. "I was lonely right next to you, and you always flinch when I touch you. As if I had no right."

Cathy tried to filter what he said through what had actually happened. She did prefer being alone with the kids. And she did turn away from him, often, because she was so angry.

"Look at my hands, Dean." Her voice shook. She held out her arms, palms up, and tried to keep them from shaking too. Her wedding band gleamed beneath the fluorescent ceiling light. He was sitting on the floor now, a few feet away, his back against the stove. "My hands have never touched anybody but you for twelve years. And before that, I don't remember really caring for anybody but you. You can't know what that feels like, can you?" She didn't let him answer. "No. Because your hands," his hands were rubbing his knees, "your hands have been on dozens of women. Before we got married and after. Every time I took the kids to Rose's for the weekend. It makes everything you touch disgusting. Including me. And that's why I turn away from you. It's so common, Dean. So damn common. I thought you were different from York Ferry boys. Better. But you're not. That's my own mistake, I guess. You're exactly like all of them, just looking to get laid on the sly. It makes me sick to my stomach."

"That's not true." He shook his head vigorously. "That's nowhere near the truth. I'm not just looking to get laid. And don't accuse me of things from before we got married. As for afterward, it was nine years before I even looked at anyone else."

"You did a lot more than look."

"All right. But don't make me such a bad guy. I didn't just want sex, although I did want that, I'll admit it. I wanted to be with someone who wouldn't jump every time I rolled over in bed and touched them. Or someone who'd sleep with me outside and look at the sky at night. You liked to do that when we were younger, but now it's as if you're afraid of getting your clothes dirty. Cathy, I'm sorry, I really am. I don't want a divorce.

I don't want to break up this family."

Why was he being so humble about it? Cathy felt uncomfortable, unsure of her previous resolve. What would happen? They'd patch everything up and just go on?

"It's not fair! You get to have everything, don't you: me, the kids, your girlfriends, and then I'm supposed to forgive you, just like that, and say, 'Oh, dear, it's fine. Let's pretend it didn't happen and try again.' And you don't hurt at all. You've already broken up this family, Dean. You just haven't noticed. For three years I've been miserable, and your eyes have been shut tight.

"Oh, I know you care about the kids. It's easy for you to care about them; you never see them. I'm not ready," she breathed deeply, "I'm not willing to just forgive you and go on as if nothing happened. You need to think long and hard about this marriage. About me. So," she let the momentum carry her along, "so I want you to move out. Maybe a separation would be good for us both."

Dean's mouth hung open. "Cath, I can't believe you. We've always lived together."

"Maybe that's part of the problem. Maybe we take each other for granted." She thought again of Dean's father, walking out on his family after fourteen years. "Or maybe we just shouldn't be married. Most people who get married as teenagers don't stay married."

"But we're not 'most people.' I don't want to live anywhere else."

"Tough. Sometimes we have to do things we don't like. You always say that to the kids, Dean."

"But what about them? When will I see them? And what will they think?"

"You can see them whenever you want to. I'm not trying to turn them against you. I know you love them. Spend Sundays with them; that's what other people do."

"One day a week?"

"That's about all you see them now."

"I can't believe this." He was looking at her with such sad eyes, practically helpless. He was shocked that she could ask him to leave. Cathy felt glad. She didn't mean to be spiteful, but she was proud of herself for taking a stand, for not succumbing. Not forgiving.

"Believe it. I want you to go tonight."

"You can't stand to be under the same roof with me for one more night?"

"Tonight, Dean."

"Where would I go?"

"That's your decision. You could stay with Joe and Fern. Or your old room at the farmhouse is probably available."

He stood up and buried his head in the jacket he had hung on the rack earlier. She wondered if he was crying. "I can't believe this," he mumbled. "I'm leaving." He didn't let her see his face.

And he went out of the kitchen and up the stairs, and Cathy heard him say good-night to the kids, then gather some clothes from the bedroom. He reappeared with his father's old suitcase and put on his jacket, laced up his boots, and grabbed his cap in the same order as always—and Cathy thought she would miss that—and, before stepping outside, he turned and asked, "Are you sure you want me to go?"

"I'm sure. Why don't you call me in a few days? Let me know where you'll be."

"Fine. I'll be at my mother's."

And he was gone.

Chapter Eleven

1978

The York Ferry IGA, though clean, lacked the dazzle and chrome of Plattsburgh's Grand Union. It contained only six aisles, where wares sometimes stood stock still for weeks, even months, accumulating dust. Knox gelatin's orange cardboard covers faded to a pasty yellow under the sun's slanting afternoon rays. Del Monte canned French-style string beans remained stuck to the aluminum shelving, the red heart beneath the company logo mocking the supermarket's unlovely decay. Joe and Kay traded feather-duster duty every morning, but their efforts failed to sway the inevitable, and on June 30, 1978, the York Ferry IGA shut its doors for the last time. The going-out-of-business sale—all items at least 50% off, some as much as 80% reduced—left the pocked linoleum floors littered with labels, wrappers, and discarded items. All of York County participated in the gutting of the store, including the Marysville mayor's wife (who drove forty miles to arrive by 8:30 a.m.); two forgotten mountain families from the nearly invisible town of Wren; the summer chef of Camp Champlain (who purchased every ice cream cone, plastic, paper goods, and ketchup bottle for back-up supplies); and Cathy Reiser Pinny, now separated from Dean, who supplemented her husband's checks with occasional work on the Lakeshore Drive. Joe was appalled to see her there along with the vultures.

"Look who just walked in," Joe said to his mother, who was ringing up items so fast her eyes never left the revolving rubber belt. Joe deposited a small bottle of Coke for Kay beside the register, flicking the cap angrily to the floor.

"Why are you so surprised? She's only human," Kay replied.

"Loyalty." Joe winced. "I thought she might have some family loyalty in the end."

"Don't be silly. She's just trying to save some money like everyone else. Go back to your counter, son."

Dragging his feet, Joe returned to the butcher area. Almost everything had disappeared from beneath the glass, including the head cheese, which generally took forever to move. (No more free slop for Fred Reber, the pig farmer, who took all edible refuse from the supermarket to feed his hogs.) Joe stood behind the smeared display case, now empty but for a roll of bologna with olives and a few portions of stew bones. Only one drop of blood spattered his white apron, which, like the butcher area itself, had been made for a taller person. Thirty-odd years before, his mother had been the butcher while the York Ferry men were at war. That bit of family history would be bulldozed along with the store.

"How's that bologna?" a woman's voice asked.

Turning from his task of sponging down the work table, Joe found Cathy, her daughter Sheila in hand, smiling tentatively.

"Well, it's half-off," Joe said. "So it must be pretty good."

"I'm so sorry about the store. What are you going to do?" Cathy pushed the moist blonde hair away from her forehead. The supermarket was hot and not air-conditioned. She told her daughter to find one small treat in the cookie section, then pushed her off in the proper direction.

Joe's hands shook as he cut off a half-pound chunk of the bologna, weighed it, wrapped it, and drew the price on the paper in black crayon. Since he was eight years old when Dean brought home his girlfriend for the first time, Joe had adored Cathy. He blamed his brother for finding her first and blamed him more for letting her go. Most York Ferry people scorned her as standoffish and hard, but Joe admired these qualities. She radiated intensity; just looking at her made Joe nervous. She wore a yellow flowered dress that matched the scarf tying her curly hair into a ponytail. He cleared his throat. "Mr. Forster was able to get me a job in P-burgh." He was embarrassed and angry over his new position; he hoped she wouldn't ask for details.

"I'm glad for you." She smiled. "When's Fern due?"

"End of summer."

"Tell her to call if she needs anything, okay?"

He nodded, wishing for the thousandth time that Fern were not pregnant just now, wishing he'd remembered to be careful instead of relying on Fern, who, sweet as she was, was not a very careful person. They'd been married not quite two years, and their tiny house across from the York Ferry Amalgamated Schools was too cramped for a family of four.

"Enjoy your bologna. And give this to Sheila." Joe fished an orange lollipop from his pocket, where he kept a supply for the children of his customers.

"Thanks. I guess one more dose of sugar couldn't possibly damage that mouthful of cavities." She waved good-bye with the packet of meat. "So long. Take good care of your wife; she'll need some extra attention these last months."

Watching her walk away, Joe bit his lips. Cathy had become much nicer to all the Pinnys since she split up with Dean. Even Kay seemed to like her lately. But Cathy would never begin to understand how he felt about her. Never.

Almost every night since Memorial Day, Joe had strapped Robert Vernon to his back and walked with Fern on the cool sand of Elbow Beach. From there they could spy on the activities of the Lakeshore Drive families, watch the stars and the lights of Vermont across the water, and feel the moist ground with their bare toes. Fern leaned against him as they walked, her short, swollen body a comfort and a burden beneath his arm. They said little; Robby slept blissfully as the sounds of a party at the huge Richardson home drifted above the still waters of the bay like the radio conversation of a late-night disc jockey filtering out the windows of a stranger's home.

"A Manhattan, please."

"Why don't they have a drink called the Montreal?" a man's high-pitched voice, heavily accented, chimed above the rest, and a chorus of laughter rippled through the group.

A dozen voices then contributed more place names for cocktails, mostly foreign, until the litany sounded like a game of Geography.

Fern patted Joe's cheek. "Wouldn't it be fun to go to Manhattan some day?"

Shrugging, Joe picked up the pace, hoping to leave such questions behind with the wisps of laughter, the Lakeshore Drive people with their trips abroad laughing at him, Joseph Pinny, who would, as of next week, serve as a meat packer and handler at the Grand Union on the mall in Plattsburgh, an invisible middleman for these wealthy consumers. A town butcher was respectable, Joe thought, a profession that made a contribution to the community. But a meat packer was a nameless, faceless worker about whom the public knew nothing and cared not at all. If only these people had shopped in York Ferry, maybe the IGA would have stayed in business.

"What's the matter, honey?" Fern stopped walking and made him look at her. "Don't worry so much, okay? We'll get along fine. I know we will."

He squeezed her fingers in response. Hopeful Fern. He'd rescued her from the transient life of an Air Force brat who would probably have become an Air Force wife, and he meant to give her a proper home and a stable life. She was a shy person, like Joe, a virgin on their wedding night, also like Joe. Yet they were intrinsically different in their approach to the future. With the failure of the IGA, York Ferry would no longer be a regular town with its own market; it was becoming a satellite of Plattsburgh and a playground for the Lakeshore Drive people, who shopped at the mall or in Albany before they arrived for the season and spent their money at the state-run liquor store, of which not a penny benefited York Ferry. They were polite enough, but to them, York Ferry people were maids, party helpers, babysitters, and handymen. Paul and Steve had done their share of dump hauls and hard labor to get summer docks out of winter storage and then dry-dock them again in September. Not Joe, who refused to give them one drop of sweat.

Somewhere out on the Richardsons' slate patio, a glass shattered, and a female voice called, "Don't worry, Sir. I'll get it."

"Was that Cathy?" Fern asked. "Sounded like her. I didn't know she was working for them."

Nor did Joe. A rush of disappointment passed through him, chilling every cell. Cathy, a servant. "I guess so. She needs money pretty bad."

"It's not *that* awful to work on the Lakeshore Drive. And the Richardsons are probably the nicest people there. You get all kinds of clothes when you work for those ladies. That's why Cathy always looks so great. I wouldn't mind having some of those fancy summer dresses, cool cotton and linen. That's the life, all right."

The regional managers of the IGA Northeastern Division had met six months earlier and agreed to consolidate. The smaller stores were losing money; the bigger markets, more centrally located, were profiting from large interstate highways like the Adirondack Northway, which had a ramp in Port Elizabeth a mere seven miles away. For the Plattsburgh and York County region, the company decided to forfeit the business from the northern part of the area to Grand Union and convert the market in New Troy, at the county's southern border, into a modern mega-store, complete with in-house bakery to serve the county government headquarters. All this was according to York Ferry store manager Averill Forster, who had pleaded for more time, more money for improvements, more attention to the special needs of his area. Forster said he could turn the market around by stocking the fancy gourmet items asked for by the summer people (French mustard, cocktail sauce, fresh shrimp, etc.) and giving the store a slick new face, as well as lowering prices on some basic goods, for which even the locals now took to the Northway to get in Plattsburgh. He was earnest, and the divisional chairman praised Forster for caring about the needs of his community (Averill told Kay, who in turn told Joe), but it was not possible. The corporation had decided to let York Ferry go.

The white, slimy substance bobbed in a briny sauce of brown liquid and pungent green stalks. There it sat, on his mother's picnic table, beside her fried chicken and Fern's potato salad and the patties ready for burgers. "Mother, what the hell is this?" Joe asked.

"Polly Brazil brought it over for us to try. She says it's the best thing since hamburger meat, only it's so much better for you. Taste it." Kay, always up for an experiment, spooned a little bit onto her paper plate and pushed the dish over to Joe. "Go on, scaredy-cat."

"Since when do you listen to Polly Brazil?" Joe was outraged. Polly Brazil and her bearded male partner (whom she never referred to as a husband) had rented the adjacent land in Madnan's Valley since 1967, when they arrived with twelve sheep and two goats in a dented yellow schoolbus converted into a house on wheels. Hippies. York Ferry had mostly ignored them, but Kay and Polly occasionally exchanged gardening information and recipes. Polly and her man were vegetarians who lived off the proceeds of the wool they raised, carded, and spun for the tourists over in Vermont. They raised chickens for eggs and drank milk from the goats, which also provided for their horrific-smelling cheese. In summer they canned and froze and dried the produce of a huge vegetable garden, and in winter, it seemed, they did nothing at all but stay in their wood-heated yellow bus-home, which never again felt the bite of asphalt beneath its wheels.

"She's a kook, Mother. Her name alone should tell you that." Their Sunday meal at the farmhouse felt tainted by the whole discussion; Joe detested even the idea of tofu.

Kay was feeding applesauce to Robbie while Fern, her cheek resting on the red-checked tablecloth, dozed in her shady corner of the picnic table. "She told me her real name is Susan Friedman, but that she left it on Long Island. Isn't that funny?" Kay said. The baby gurgled, and Kay made silly faces before kissing his brow. "Robby thinks it's very funny, don't you, sweetheart?"

Exasperated, Joe could only frown at his mother and son. A food to replace meat. Was that what Robby would grow up to eat? And the next child too? He put a dab of the tofu-and-scallion mixture on his tongue and then spat it out onto the grass. "Yuck!"

He felt ignored. Extricating himself with some difficulty from the picnic bench—he had quite a potbelly these days—he decided to walk the periphery of the Pinny property, a habit he'd begun unconsciously as a child and now indulged every time he came out to the farm, even in winter. Nineteen acres of prime valley soil, bought and paid for by his absent father. A wooden farmhouse from 1880, needing repair but still solid underneath the peeling paint, the property was everything to Joe. He loved this place more passionately than the rest of the family put together. As far as Joe was concerned, he had no father at all but the land itself, the view down to Lake Champlain and the afternoon shadows from Madnan's Ridge, the great Green Mountains framing the morning sun far to the east. On the southern tip of the land, an old hay harvester lay rotting and rusting under a tangle of blackberry vines. He tried a berry but it wasn't yet ripe. Two rabbits scampered by him toward the narrow brook that demarcated the eastern end of the Pinny parcel. The stream flowed all the way down the mountains from Miner's

Peak before losing its force and breadth to deposit a trickle of cold water into Lake Champlain.

Joe rubbed his belly, big from beer and too much potato salad, too many macaroni and cheese dinners. His mother had already invited him and his family to live up at the farm with her. What did she need all this space to herself for? she'd asked. Paul came and went at whim, but there was certainly room enough for any of the children and grandchildren. Fern, however, had refused. She couldn't live in her mother-in-law's house, she'd insisted. It wasn't possible. So they had filled to the brim their little house with bodies and babies and magazines and formula bottles, Joe feeling cramped and claustrophobic whenever he was home. The Bouquet ran behind their property, cooling things down in the summer but bringing with it black flics, mosquitoes, and pencil snakes, scattered litter washing up on the shores of their back yard. Joe spent too much time already keeping the garbage off their land. And now, another baby.

As Joe fretted and paced the hospital lobby, Fern's labor so protracted and difficult that the doctors were considering performing a Caesarean-section, he thought about praying. A laminated Lord's Prayer hung on the wall above a tableful of glossy magazines, just below a hanging plant of spidering ivy. He might have missed it in the lobby's clutter, but Joe hadn't. Only his grandmother had had what he would call religious belief, though Joe described it as steel will rather than "Makerfaith," as old Eleanor termed it. She had died the opening day of the Adirondack Northway, killed by a drunk, along with a whole car of church women on their way to do volunteer work at this very hospital. How would she have reconciled that way of dying with her faith? Joe read through the Lord's Prayer again, convinced that the deep thread of fear in his gut was attached only to the superstitious part of his brain, that the adrenaline-laced panic propelling his race around and around the lobby had no place in this chrome and fluorescent world. Fern had had one fine pregnancy already, one healthy boy, yet he was afraid now; it had been fifteen hours; he began to hyperventilate. He looked down at his pudgy hands, still stained with grease from the meat hoist; his work boots, too, bore the remnants of the day's efforts in the meat-cutting area. He felt isolated. The whirring voices over the intercom sounded like some garbled TV medical show. The orange and plastic benches were unnatural and foreign; the hanging plant, he discovered upon examination, was plastic, too, its fronds sprightly reaching in perpetual health. A cruel joke perpetrated by the hospital management: featuring benches and plants that never wore, never grew tired and old, never fell to pieces the way humans did.

A nurse informed him that the situation was still the same, the obstetrician holding off the C-section for just a few minutes more. He made his way to a telephone booth.

"Nothing to report yet, Mom. I just have this bad feeling. Something. I don't know. Like something scary."

"Honey, go walk around the block. The air will make you feel better." Kay cooed something to the baby which Joe couldn't make out, and then, "Daddy, it's your Daddy, Robby. Can you say hello? Hello, Daddy." But Robby remained silent, and Joe promised he would call again soon.

Daddy. It still shocked him to hear himself referred to by that word, that term of love that meant a whole universe of things, so many of which contained responsibility, duty, patience, tolerance. These qualities, he imagined, were essential to make a good father. Certainly his own had had none of them, at least not after Zoe Mae was born, precipitating his disappearance. Perhaps before that Vernon had been dutiful; in fact, Joe had never heard otherwise. His father was said to have been a hard worker, a good mechanic, a thrifty economizer, all qualities Joe himself embodied. The paid-off mortgage on the farmhouse and land were proof. But they were not enough to counter the lack, the great gap of Vernon's absence. When Joe turned eighteen, he spent a week or two plotting a search-and-rescue mission for Vernon. He would find his father, weak but alive, where he had been chained to a wall, force-fed, held against his will by some psycho in Canada for all these years of no word or post-card or the slightest glimmer of communication. Joe could laugh at himself now, a father for the second time at the age of twenty-three, for his grandiose teenager's idea of heroism. His father, after all, was a war hero. Perhaps they shared that, too. What could make a man walk out on his family? Anything at all, Joe concluded: a plastic fern in a lobby or a drop of calf's blood on the tip of one's boot.

Joe took Kay's advice and walked around the hospital area. The autumn night had turned brisk, and he could see his breath in the air, blunting the edge of his panic. He watched an ambu-lance scream into the emergency entrance and unload a child, a tiny girl who looked dead but must have had some possibility of survival since they were rushing her in as fast as they could. Someone was still hoping. A ragged looking young woman with a black eye emerged from the ambulance under the harsh out-door lights and limped after the girl, who must have been her daughter. Joe wondered again about his grandmother, who somehow managed to make sense of the world from her read-ings of the Bible and an amalgamation of common sense and strongheadedness. She had been so mangled by the truck driver that the family had not been allowed to see her body.

William Lee Pinny was born early the next morning, small, jaundiced, with an undersized heart. The doctors said his condi-tion was extremely rare, and Joe got the impression the team of specialists was excited about having such an unusual case on their hands. Doctors from all over flew in to see Billy. When Joe looked at him for the first time, it was clear the boy would not live long. Robby had been nearly twice his size at birth, yowling, punching the air with angry energy. Billy just lay there, his skin a ghostly yellow. Fern couldn't look at him without crying, and after a few weeks of visiting the baby in the hospital every day, she took to stopping at the York Ferry Inn on her way home. In alcohol she rediscovered her earlier optimism.

The butcher at the Grand Union lost a hand to the grinder in a freak accident, and Joe was moved up to take his position. On an afternoon when he was gutting chickens for packages of hearts, gizzards, and livers, he was summoned to the counter by the buzz of the customer button. Exchanging his bloody apron for a clean one, he went out of the back room to find Cathy and Sheila looking lost in the huge "Meat Products" wing of the super-store.

"Joe, do you have a minute?" Cathy sent her daughter to await her at the end of the aisle after Joe nodded reluctantly. "I know my relationship to your family is kind of awkward right now, but I do want to help. Please. If there's anything I can do. Please call me."

Biting his lip, Joe mumbled his thanks. What could she do that could happen in his lifetime? Start their lives over again? There was nothing. He would never tell her how he felt. Maybe she knew, maybe she did, but she would return only sympathy, compassion for his passion. Every time he saw her, a horrible gouging pain appeared as if it were the first time, all the air knocked out of his lungs. It had grown worse since she was no longer with Dean. Cathy repeated her willingness to help, then backed away.

"Good-bye, Uncle Joe," Sheila called, and they disappeared into the brightly lit, cavernous market.

Joe returned to his chickens and the terrible task of severing hearts from their rightful bodies.

Chapter Twelve

1979

More than anything, she loved a horizon with nothing on it. Shadows clutter York Ferry, memory occupying every corner and field. Out here, looking east over the Atlantic, she could testify that nothing had ever happened to harm her. The gray sky offered no evidence of past acts, nor the gray sea, indistinguishable from air. Her father's absence bore a slow hole in her heart, but here even absence did not exist. History evaporated at sea. Every sailor with something to forget or remember could see and sense only water, sky, ship. On the huge Coast Guard cruiser, the life of the shore diminished, sifted by salt winds, never quite disappearing.

Zoe Mae was spending her afternoon off, as she always did, on the foredeck with a book, today only half-interested in reading as she tried to clear her mind of business. The second mate's duties proved overwhelming at times: tedium, drain, imagined and real responsibility for other lives. She studied the small print of the ratty paperback, willing her mind to depart the deck for the tidy, foreign world of Miss Marple's England, the mystery of the place as intriguing as the detective's task.

Suddenly Charlayne appeared, her sturdy brown arm sliding down the rail toward the open book. "Hey there, sweet. Thought I'd check and make sure none of the boys were coveting that delicious body of yours." After checking to make sure no one could see them, she leaned over and kissed a freckle on Zoe Mae's cheek, her strong hand pressing Zoe Mae's butt. "Well, coveting's okay in itself, but doing something about it is another story." She winked.

"Charlayne! You have to be more careful up here!" Appalled and exhilarated by Charlayne's brazenness, Zoe Mae smiled nervously, her body aswim with the contradictory reactions Charlayne's presence elicited: longing, indifference, disgust, anger, desire. The older woman opened a pack of generic menthol cigarettes and offered one, as she always did, to Zoe Mae, who shook her head disapprovingly. "Cancer sticks. It's a shame, beautiful girl like you." She said that every time Charlayne lit up.

To Zoe Mae, Charlayne's beauty transcended all preordained categories. She stood 5'10", with a slim bottom half and small breasts, but her arms were steel: solid biceps of a dimension Zoe Mae would never achieve, no matter how much weight she lifted. The daughter of sugarcane pickers from Florida, Charlayne worked in the engine room and took slack from no one. Four years ago she had adopted Zoe Mae into an intense and loyal friendship, protecting her as an older sibling would from dangers actual and impending. She was, in fact, ten years older than Zoe Mae, the same age as Dean. For the last eleven months, they had been lovers, Zoe Mae slowly losing her resistance and succumbing to Charlayne's patient, enveloping embrace. Still, she didn't know how she felt about it from day to day, her desire and need for love crashing headlong into an idealized vision of some handsome man, white though faceless, whose arms opened toward her, encircling Zoe Mae's smallness like a natural harbor rescuing a storm-tossed sailboat. "Be mine," he was saying: "I'll never leave you." He would smell like a man—or as Zoe Mae imagined an adult male should smell—responsible, dependable, faintly sour. No matter how much Charlayne sweated, she wore the aroma of talc, the smell of mother and baby at once.

Zoe Mae watched the broad, callused hand that rose to grasp

the cigarette and fling it over the side in one sure, graceful gesture. They both followed it with their eyes as it sailed in a falling arc. Once, Zoe Mae had thought of herself as tough, someone to be reckoned with back in York Ferry, but she didn't know what toughness required until she joined the Coast Guard and met Charlayne and the other women. Zoe Mae was unacquainted with her own ignorance until that first year at sea when it seemed every man and woman wanted something from her: straight or gay, married, unmarried, old enough to be her father, or mother. And the physical exhaustion: she'd fallen asleep over dinner almost every night. But the rest were never too tired to want. She was confounded by all of it: the intensity of desire in men and women long confined on ship, the commonness of homosexuality, the vehemence of friendship. Loyalties solidified in a week, a night. Hatred rose like sea foam, cresting into violence when communication failed, flinging itself flat on some port shore, spent only by fists and a last exhalation of energy. Her life back in York Ferry appeared a distant dream, a sleeping preparation for the life to follow.

"I'll see you supper time. And later. Second mate, Sir!" Laughing, Charlayne saluted for the benefit of a few men who had appeared on deck. She pursed her lips and feigned a small kiss before heading below.

Unfolding a letter from her mother, Zoe Mae scanned the familiar handwriting which, however neat and careful, slanted in opposite directions, the top half looking nothing like the bottom, the letters veering every which way. The North Country changed little from letter to letter. It turned on its axis, shifting the angle at which it received the sun like any other place, people aging, withering, at times jolted by violence. Her grandmother's death, when Zoe Mae was twelve, had rocked her sense of surety, had shaken the world from its poles. Instantaneous death, the sheriff had said, but Zoe Mae believed her grandmother knew fear before she died, the hollow terror of the inevitable. Zoe Mae remembered perfectly such fear. Not long before graduation, she and Eric, her high school beau, had left a party drunk, she less so than he, but he insisted on driving. They weren't going far, so she didn't worry. Driving south around Elbow Curve, they crossed the yellow line into the lights of a pickup. Only miraculous alertness on the part of the other driver had prevented all their deaths. She remembered most the silence: no horns, no screaming, just a split second of outrage passing in terrible quiet. She would never trust Eric again, and gladly broke off the relationship when she left York Ferry.

Dear Zoe Mae,

This will have to be short because I'm tired from looking after Robby and the baby, who doesn't seem to get any better no matter how much medicine they pour into him up at Plattsburgh General. Fern gets so upset after bringing him home from treatment that she goes up to the inn to have a beer, leaving me to watch them both. "For half an hour," she says, then comes back two hours later, glassy-eyed and happy, by which time Joe's back from work, and either me or him better make dinner because I wouldn't trust her near a hot stove.

I still feel sad that old Herkimer isn't here to sit on my feet and drool. But it's nice to be alone in the house. Paul's out somewhere—he's been gone three days. Thunder's rattling the panes. You and I both love the storms. I've built a fire in the woodstove, and I'm drinking tea with milk and sugar, like Grandma used to make. It'd be nice if you were here. Sometimes I look in your room to see if old Ramona is stirring up any dust. Remember how long it took you to let go of her—I was ready to worry there was something wrong with you.

I wish you'd come home more often. I've tried to be the patientest mother in the world, but once a year is way too little to see your own family. You mentioned that you and your friend Charlayne go exploring when you're on shore. Well, how about a little North Country exploration? I bet she's never seen this corner of the country. Bring her along—you know there's plenty of room for your friends here.

Averill asked me to marry him, again, and I said no, again. I don't understand why he can't be content with this nice thing we have together. He says it's for my benefit—that he wants me to be well taken care of when he dies, but I don't want to run my life that way. It's like waiting around for death. Besides, I'm just starting to get along with Simon, who I'm guessing will hang around his father's house for a long time. He doesn't want me to marry his dad.

Well, pumpkin-head, your old Mom's getting sloppy. The sound of the rain against the big window is putting me to sleep. Remember what I said: Christmas is a long ways away. And I order you to telephone me the next time you're on shore.

Love and invisible hugs from Ramona.

Mom

Zoe Mae didn't want to take Charlayne home with her. Not yet. Showing York Ferry to Charlayne—and vice versa—signified something major, an announcement she wasn't ready to make.

Dear Mom,

I'd like to come home before Christmas, but I can't say it's actually possible. I hate flying, hate being more than a mile away from water—on the ground, that is. But you definitely succeeded in making the farmhouse sound cozy and appealing. I can't hear the rain fall from my cabin. It's too far below deck. I miss that.

Funny that you mentioned Ramona. I haven't thought about her in years. I guess I felt deprived that the boys got to have a bunch of brothers and a sister too, but I had not even one sister. So I invented a girl who would keep me company when I was tired of being with boys. She liked everything I did. Actually, Charlayne is fun to hang around with, although we're not alike at all.

When I get into port this weekend, I'll find out about flying home from the next port, which is around Thanksgiving. I promise to call, but I can't guarantee a visit.

155

Why don't you let someone else do the babysitting at Joe's? Don't get all run down because things are tough over there. I'm sad and mad to hear that Fern's drinking. And since when does Paul go off on a three-day binge? Don't cave in to Averill, whatever you do. I mean, do what you want to when you're good and ready. Grandma never let anyone push her around. I know she drove you crazy a lot, but she was a tough old gal. I admire her more and more as I get older. I'll ask Charlayne if she wants to come at Christmas, but she'll probably want to be with her Mom in Florida.

Hugs to everyone, esp. you and Dean.

Love,
Zoe Mae

If Charlayne were a man, Zoe Mae thought, she *would* invite her for Christmas. She couldn't argue that Charlayne had treated her similarly. Every month, Charlayne suggested a trip to Florida, repeating that her mother would be pleased to meet her. When Charlayne's father died not long ago, her mother moved in with a woman friend. Charlayne thought they might be lovers, but nothing had been said.

That night in their bunk, Charlayne brought up the subject. "I'd bring you home 'cause I'm proud of you," Charlayne said. "But you're not proud of me, are you? Maybe it's fine to get your hands dirty at sea, but not in your white bread countryhouse."

Furious, Zoe Mae wrestled out from under her covers and scrambled up to Charlayne's bed. "That's bullshit, Boyce! It's not your color that makes me uptight."

"Oh, right. It's what I got between my legs that's the problem."

Her legs dangling over the edge, Zoe Mae rested her head on her knees, embarrassed. "It's not a problem what's between your legs—between my legs, for that matter—but I'm just not sure I'm a lesbian. I mean, I never thought about women until I met you." Lesbian. The word sounded so harsh, so final, as if she'd named herself the victim of a chronic disease, an epileptic or a diabetic.

"Four years this woman's arms been around you, comforting you, making love to you, and you're not a lesbian. Right." Charlayne had raised herself to her elbows, and her voice rose with indignation. "How long I spent consoling you over that dumb-ass Jack or those other stupid white boys you thought you wanted? Shit. I'm the dumb-ass here."

"Charlayne, we did *not* spend four years as lovers. It's been one year. Almost. You were my friend before that, doing what friends do for each other."

"Well, you got a loose definition of friendship. 'Just friends' don't spend that much time together, don't stand so close together. You were hungry for me, Zoe Mae, from the goddamn beginning."

"I didn't know you were so resentful about it. Or were you trying to get into my pants the whole time?"

Silence.

"You don't believe that," Charlayne said.

"Maybe I fill the Coast Guard's female quota, and you fill the black quota, and I fill your white girl quota." Zoe Mae trembled, her bare feet ice cold. She'd never thought about the two of them in that way, but there was something about their attraction, an electric illicitness, that had to do with how completely opposite they were.

Charlayne's arm reached out to find Zoe Mae's knee, her fingertip drawing a slow spiral on her kneecap. It gave Zoe Mae the chills, made her stomach tense up, and as Charlayne's hand traveled lightly up her thigh, beneath her T-shirt to her breast, her nipples hardened.

"But you like me getting into your pants, don't you."

It was not a question, and Zoe Mae did not bother to answer.

Charlayne pulled Zoe Mae down so that she was lying on top of her. She kissed Charlayne's tobacco-tasting lips, trying to take back her words, kissing away the smell of coffee and old bitterness, swallowed one more time. In spite of everything, Zoe Mae believed, Charlayne—unlike her father—would never let her go.

Skagway, Alaska

Dec. 1

Dear Kay,

It's my 56th birthday today, and I have vowed to stop deceiving you and me both. All these years I've been waiting for a signal from you so that I could give up and come home. You were the semaphore and I the headlong train, barreling through on some unworkable notion of righting past wrongs. I'm not sure if I wanted you to forgive me for leaving in the first place, or if it was an unconditional guarantee of love I was hoping for. But there was no signal at all. I pretended you were mulling this over, and I granted you a lot of time as it had taken me many years to know why I'd left. After a while, I let you take over. I no longer felt comfortable with the idea of walking back in the same brash way I walked out.

You're ready to turn 60. I'll bet we have some grandchildren by now. What will you do? I'd like to retire to York Ferry. The vastness of the Yukon no longer thrills me. At times, I am frightened by it. I feel I don't exist here, don't take up any room. I remember the soft green of Madnan's Ridge at this time of year, the small comfort of it, and the way the Bouquet River bubbles up around the bridgeposts in town. I'd like to come home to the place where I was raised, though you may not want me there. I'll certainly understand if you've found someone else and don't want me to share the house where we raised the children, the land I tilled for all those years. We are, after all, still husband and wife. I have a right to be home. All these years I thought it was me with the power to come or go, but it was you, all this time, determining everything.

Irene died a long time ago, and I see now that I have wasted a lifetime pondering the past, blaming myself for failing to save her. The children have grown up without me. When I was with them, I was hardly present. I am an old man with old memories, failing my dead lover and my living wife and children. I could never forgive myself. Maybe it's time. I will spend a few months here wrapping up my business affairs, and then I'll set out for home.

Vernon

Chapter Thirteen

1980

The first to hear was Kay, who, while getting dressed the morning of March 16th, picked up the phone expecting to find Averill's voice greeting her and the day but listened instead to a stranger asking if she was Mrs. Vernon Pinny. Is that who she is? Kay nodded dumbly, but the man asked again, and she had to affirm it aloud. Then she heard what she had always known she would hear from a stranger. He referred to "the deceased," a war hero in a war thirty-odd years before who was now dead in a V.A. hospital in the state of Washington, and if she was indeed Mrs. Vernon Pinny of the Short Bay Road, York Ferry, New York, as the emergency papers deemed proper to notify, they would fly his body home to her that day. The man regretted being the bearer of bad news. He hated delivering these messages, although it was his job, the voice added conspiratorially, but he needed her permission for she was, he assumed, the closest living family member of "the deceased."

Twenty years ago Vernon had packed a duffel bag and lifted his feet in the slow, methodical manner he had of walking out the door to the dirt drive, where, instead of to work, his feet took him to the station and he waited there only fifteen minutes for the train to Montreal. That morning, warm and smelling of the lake, clicked into the spools of Kay's memory and froze, a sepia photograph of an old man—no, a young man, only thirty-seven—winding down from the white, peeling porch and saluting the house before marching onward. No. She had no such memory, only a dream of it, since Kay had been inside feeding the twins and Zoe Mae as she had every morning when they were all small (Kay pictured herself almost as small as the children) and filled every seat around the breakfast table. The yellow curtains probably blew over the baby in her high chair, and whenever Kay tried to move her out of harm's way, Zoe Mae would gesture no! She loved to grab the tip of sunny chintz and put it in her mouth, rub it over her cheeks and lips. Had Kay looked out, then, beneath the raised curtain to see her husband leave for the last time? She wasn't positive. And there was something wrong with this image: wouldn't she have noticed the duffel bag? How could he have left without her observing such an obvious statement of departure? And it was three miles to the depot. No. He had worn his work clothes like any other day and thoughtfully chewed his toast, ate a fried egg with habitual care, cleaned his plate, swallowed the last of the coffee, and kissed her faintly on the forehead, kissed the children, then walked out the door to his pickup. Was the duffel in the truck already? Had he stopped at the shed to sneak it into the passenger's seat? For how many months or years had he planned his leavetaking?

Kay didn't know any of these answers. It was so long ago she might have invented everything, including the blue lake smell of a ripe June morning, how the twins would hit each other, in a friendly way, every day at breakfast, and Zoe Mae playing with the kitchen curtain, pulling it aside as if the world out the window were a spectacle, and Kay the spectator.

What she knew was that she was standing in the living room with a dead phone in her hand, barefoot, sweater dangling from an elbow. She sat on the floor, cradling the receiver before returning it to the rickety telephone table beside the couch. The house was so quiet she could hear her own breathing: short, fast breaths which sounded too ragged, too ravaged, to be her own.

Vernon was dead, and Kay was alive to acknowledge that she

was still, it was true, Mrs. Vernon Pinny. She would drive to Plattsburgh Air Force Base late that afternoon to recover the body of a man she once knew, the decorated veteran who voluntarily discharged himself from the post of father and husband for something Kay would not or could not understand. She lay back on the rug and stared up at the ceiling. She had never lain on her back this early in the day and examined the living room ceiling, which was yellowing and in need of paint. It seemed to breathe with her, the corners lifting like flaps on envelopes, hinting of secrets inside or underneath, a blank notepad awaiting the scrawl of revelation.

Holding her hands, palms out, above her face, as if to shield herself from light, Kay eyed the thin wedding band she'd never removed, veins of work and age crisscrossing forearms to fingers, knobby knuckles, hands that hoisted a thousand, maybe a million sacks of groceries for York Ferry people and lifted her five babies up and down so often she'd wondered her back hadn't cracked in half. Instead it had grown limber and supple, Kay of the hard hands and strong back, hands that sowed gardens and reaped sunflowers would now touch for the final time the man she had touched and touched for fourteen years, his neck and hips and penis and lips, the Vernon of her youth, together the young parents of a glowing family now all grown, for better and worse, and Vernon had missed it all, missed the coming of age of five fleshy beings, his own blood pulsing through every one of them, bidden, unbidden.

The hands collapsed, unable to remain aloft. She was conscious of a tiny knot of pain, a pit like the core of a golfball or a globe deep inside her chest, thudding as it grew, but she could not reach it and take it out to examine. She feared that if she failed to unravel its strands at once, they would fester forever, breaching her at inappropriate times and places, making her the woman she might have become these twenty years had she let herself be dragged down into the pit of despair that fully acknowledged that Vernon, in a conscious and premeditated way, had deserted her and her children for a dead girl and an impalpable idea of honor.

Coughing, sputtering, she found herself in a near fit, choking as if she had swallowed something rancid. Tears rose unsummoned as she convulsed there on the living room floor, white hair billowing around her face, the yellow sweater still attached to one arm now serving as a handkerchief into which she coughed pieces of phlegm or the lining of her throat, spitting twenty years' dormancy, all the stuff of her, long in hibernation now birthing in great rage.

When Dean heard his name, amplified, announced by the front desk receptionist at county headquarters, he knew something horrible had happened. Rolling out from beneath a service vehicle, nearly tripping a co-worker with his long legs, he scrambled to his feet and ran for the office, heartbeats like buckshot firing too fast. His children, his mother, his sister and brothers; in this order he worried about their fate, names flashing with accompanying faces as if he were identifying bodies in a morgue, as he had seen on TV crime shows. Little Dean, Sheila; Kay; Zoe Mae; Steve, Paul, Joe. When he arrived at the receptionist's desk, he realized he had omitted Cathy from his list.

"Son. Oh, Dean." His mother's voice faltered, garbling her next words. He had never heard this tone.

"Mom! Are you all right?"

"Your father, Dean. Your father..." is dead. He finished the sentence along with her silently, lips moving.

"My father is dead," he said to the receptionist, a young woman with whom he once spent the night, a Susan or Suzanne who stopped typing mid-sentence to meet his eyes, mouth open, her hand over her heart in instant empathy.

"I don't want to go alone for the body."

Light turned thick in the fluorescently lit office.

"Of course, Mom. I'll go with you. Do you want me to come now?"

162

Susan/Suzanne bit her pink nails and glanced at the base of the phone, where clear buttons flashed orange with increasing frequency. She made a don't-rush gesture, assuring him the calls would wait, but Dean had finished, and he handed her the receiver gingerly, as if it were a foreign object.

"Tell White I'm taking the rest of the day. Probably tomorrow, too." His voice dropped to a hoarse whisper. "My father is dead." How peculiar to say "my father" to a stranger, to anyone. Susan/Suzanne leaned over her desk as if she'd like to hug him but couldn't decide if the embrace was appropriate, for she had recently married. Dean felt kindly toward her, benevolent, fatherly, and patted her shoulder as if it were she who had suffered the loss. "It's okay, Sue. It's okay. I haven't seen my father in twenty years. It doesn't really get to me." He heard himself lying and abruptly left.

Out the door and through the long maintenance garage to the parking lot, legs propelling him forward in a half-run, half-gallop, he found he could breathe best by taking short, shallow swallows, inhaling and exhaling in bursts of pain. Starting the Jeep with sharp, jerky movements, as if his nervous system had somehow blown a fuse, Dean drove the back streets of New Troy in a blur, until he braked suddenly in the middle of the road. "Just me now. Just me." The words spoke themselves, but he didn't understand. "Old man, the old man—I'm the old man." Of course he had always been the old man. Since the morning of his father's departure, when Dean was only thirteen, the responsible old man, a teenager, carving the ham, handing his paychecks to Kay without once considering not to, Dean the old man at thirty-three, a divorced father of two with too many women slept with to count, he realized he was still that adolescent, listening patiently to his mother telling him his father had gone, telling him as if he were a grown man, asking his advice. She ruined his life!

Horns honked, breaking the reverie, triggering his fury. "Asshole!" he yelled out the window, aware it was he who was blocking traffic. "Asshole!" He kept shouting but didn't move the Jeep, and when a large man in overalls got out of the pickup behind him, glowering, Dean comprehended that it was Vernon he should blame: not Kay but his father who stole his youth.

At the York Ferry Inn, George Reiser and Paul played gin, smoked cigarettes and drank Wild Turkey in a synchronized, silent dance of hands, the colors and numbers on the cards fading into the general dimness. Paul played by rote, embraced in the comforting haze of alcohol, the two men nodding at the table in a circle of light which leaked in from the half-shuttered windows. A cigarette dropped its cylinder of ash into his lap, a ghostly caterpillar, and Paul blinked himself awake just as George spread his cards in victory. Smiling, Paul gestured at his opponent to deal again; he always lost at cards, expected to lose and play again and again, no matter how far in debt he fell, and today, the continuation of last night, his debts had risen so high around him that the men no longer paid attention, secure in their boozy slough. They'd forgotten how many drinks and how many games, and though it was nearing 11 a.m., Paul had just noticed another day had begun. He poured the last of the bottle into his glass, nodded at George in acknowledgment to the victor by the defeated, and drank. George, however, had begun to snore, open-mouthed.

Outside, the light hurt Paul's eyes. Too much brightness for a hungover drunk, he thought, and vaguely remembered losing his sunglasses, somewhere, not long ago. One foot in front of the other, worn tennis shoes progressing down the pavement. No matter how drunk, Paul could walk; his feet took him home from women's houses and the York Ferry Inn, the more distant Champlain Bar & Grill, from Dean's railroad apartment or Joe's crowded rental by the school, Paul had walked miles and miles home to the farmhouse, where his mother smiled sadly and forgave and forgave, urging him to sleep, feeding him when he woke. Smelling woodstove smoke and the odor of gasoline as he followed the trail beside Route 22, Paul left town for the open countryside. His thin jeans jacket failed to warm him, and he remedied the chill with a pint of brandy kept for emergencies of weather like this one.

Tires squealed and slowed on the opposite side of the road. Paul looked up to see Dean watching him from the Jeep, staring as if Paul were some goddamn wino. "Quit looking at me like that. Go on! I didn't ask for a ride." He was too drunk to really yell, and his pathetic attempt saddened him deeply.

"Get in, Paul." Dean continued his unwavering gaze, the look on his face disgust or contempt, or pity mixed with both.

"Why do you act like you're so much better than me, Dean?"

"Get in the Jeep. I have some news for you."

Nausea began, a slow discomfort in the gut as he crossed the road, misjudging the speed of an approaching car which swerved to the shoulder to avoid him, the driver shaking his fist, cursing him through the shut window. Paul yelled, "Son of a bitch!" and wondered what Dean was doing here in the middle of the day. Something ominous had happened, something expected but feared, like the very last sip from the last bottle in the house, the end of the end. Inside the Jeep he steadied his hand with a swallow of brandy. "Want some?"

Shaking his head, Dean engaged the gears, looking straight in front of him, lips drawn tight.

As they bounced along the highway, Paul's nausea settled into an almost pleasant rhythm; he was so accustomed to feeling sick that he believed himself comfortable. His head lolled against the headrest. He had forgotten how he shouted at Dean, forgot that Dean had something to tell him, so he was surprised when his brother pulled off the Short Bay Road and stopped, cutting the engine before they arrived at the farmhouse.

"How drunk are you?"

"Is this a test?" Paul laughed. "Drunk enough to see double but not drunk enough to fall over? Drunk as a skunk? Sunk, sunk, sunk."

"Shut up." Dean wouldn't look at him, staring instead into his lap, heavy hands intertwining.

"You're turning gray as an old workhorse, brother. You'll be white like Mom if you don't get laid more often." Grinning at his joke, Paul surveyed the valley covered in winter's gray, wide fields reduced to the nubby stubble of a hobo's cheeks, skeletal trees clawing the sky, and now the promise of rain. Was the landscape ugly or beautiful, he wondered. Both. His brother, too, he decided, was ugly and beautiful, sitting there passing judgment on him, as righteously responsible as ever. It had always been this way, yet Paul, resenting him, admired him as well: the sure step, the never-ever sloppy drunk, the come-on lines which did not fail to get the girl. Dean once persuaded sisters to sleep with them, Canadian twins passing through York Ferry, lost on the scenic route between Montreal and Manhattan.

"Vernon's dead. Died of a heart attack, last night, in Seattle." Dean's voice was flat, betraying no more emotion than if he were a newsman broadcasting the toll from traffic accidents, a grim but anonymous statistic of chance.

"Vernon Pinny, you mean? Dad? Formerly known as our father?" Sarcasm sprang reflexively, Paul's grin degenerating into a smirk.

"That's the one." Dean finally turned to face him. "You're jealous because I knew him a little; you've always been jealous. It wasn't up to me, you know, being the first."

Opening the door, Paul retched onto the dirt. The results of three days' alcohol with only one real meal spilled out of him silently; he was used to it, but usually the sickness announced itself with more warning. Finished, he wiped his mouth with the back of his hand.

"Jesus, Paul," Dean murmured. "Jesus Christ."

"The king is dead. Long live the king!" Paul smiled then felt sick again. Father of the lost letter, lost love, the lost father who lost him, Paul, and the rest of them, on purpose. "I'm glad he's dead. It's about time. Our father, who art in heaven. No, I hope he's not."

"Shut your fucking mouth. You're in worse shape than I realized. Goddamn alcoholic."

"What are you? You just hold it better. You cover your ass better."

"Bullshit. I'm no drunk."

"Excuse me, Mr. Upstanding Citizen, Sir." Paul saluted.

The brothers sat in silence, hands on their knees, the windshield spattered at last with the day's first rain.

After his son had died two months before, Joe took up smoking, and he was on a cigarette break, lighting his second in the loading dock, when his partner yelled out the vented window that he had a phone call. Reluctantly, he flicked the burning Pall Mall as far as he could, rubbed his hands together, and entered the frigid butcher shop. The grinder was grinding, stainless steel teeth rhythmically ripping beef to burger.

"Can you shut that off for a minute?" he shouted.

The machine slowed to a stop, and Joe lifted the receiver to his ear, trembling slightly. He did not get calls at work very often. Since the telephone rang with the news that Billy's heart had stopped, he figured there could be no worse calls.

"Joseph?"

"What is it, Mom?" There was no answer. "You okay? Robby and Fern okay?"

"They're fine. There's nothing to worry about, but..." She cleared her throat, and in the wordless seconds which followed, Joe intuited what had happened, who had died.

"Your father, Joseph, passed away in a veteran's hospital in Seattle. They're flying his body back this afternoon."

"Oh." His throat constricting, he swallowed hard. Who was this father, now dead? He didn't know how to feel. "Do you want me to come home?" Funny how he automatically used "home" for the farmhouse when he'd lived with Fern in town for four years.

167

"It's up to you. Dean's here. He'll go with me to get...the body. Paul came home; he's sleeping now. We'll try to have the funeral tomorrow." Kay paused, and her faltering voice recovered some of its usual force. "I have to get a hold of your sister, somehow, and I haven't been able to reach Steve."

Joe imagined Steve swinging on a hammock between two tall pines, playing guitar for the deer. "You try at camp?"

"Nobody answers. I guess I'll keep calling."

"I'll quit work and go get him. It could be days before he gets to a phone. He's probably camping." Although Joe and Steve rarely talked at length, Joe understood his hermit brother best.

"In the rain?"

"He camps in the snow, Mom."

"Okay. You find him and bring him home."

The first clear emotion Joe could identify was that he was happy to leave work for the day. Lately his job had become intolerable. When he worked at the IGA, butchering had seemed a respectable, even honorable profession, but all the mechanization made him feel like a machine himself, and he no longer took pride in his position. He'd have liked to do something new but didn't know what. And the bills from the hospital kept on coming.

Tossing his apron in the hamper, he said, "Sorry, Lloyd, but I've got to take off. My old man died, and I have to find my brother Steve out in the woods."

His partner shook his head, mouth twisted in commiseration. "Man, you've had one bad year. I'm sorry to hear it, Joe. Real sorry." He extended his hand, and the men shook, black and white skin alike dry and cracked from handling frozen meat.

"Thanks. But this is nothing compared to my son. Haven't seen my father in twenty years. I don't really remember him."

"Yeah, but still. Good luck, man."

The smell of his pine bough fire soothed Steve, assuring him of the season's progress from the pureness of winter to the eruption of spring. For over a decade, Steve had lived this way, a year-round resident of Camp Champlain: caretaker, plumber, man-of-all-tasks. Whenever weather permitted, he fished and camped in a secluded cove not far from the main buildings; he'd built a lean-to out of scrap wood from where he could watch his bobber in the lake, even as the rain fell. The fire sputtered, hissing in protest as the force of the drops increased. He would not catch many fish today, if any. Already he had checked the cabins and outbuildings for signs of damage by animals or vandals, the restless teenagers from Port Elizabeth, and found the mailbox empty: no chores invented by the owner to keep him busy with inventory. Sometimes he read, or practiced the guitar, which he had been teaching himself to play the last few years. He saw no one, and though he listened to the radio, he did not own a television, did not care to be reminded of the chaos outside his hermitage.

The rustle in the leaves, then, he attributed to a raccoon or chipmunk and was not afraid.

"Steve! You back there? I smelled the fire."

Joe appeared beneath the arms of a giant fir, clad in a glistening rain slicker. The fire spat, and Steve's red bobber waltzed on the waves in a frenzy of rain.

"Nice shelter. When'd you build this?" Without asking permission, Joe entered and sat beside him on the crude, low bench. "Pretty cold in here, though."

Steve cleared his throat several times before he could respond; a few days had passed since he went to town for supplies and had even a minimal conversation with anyone. He called home infrequently, and then only to appease Kay.

"Two years ago. What are you doing here?" Upon asking the question, Steve realized how much he resented the rupture of his solitude, this noisy intrusion a shock to his system.

Shaking off the wet, Joe got up and stood at the edge of the shelter, peering at the distant shore of Vermont, which was barely visible through the rain. "You ever been over there?"

"Once."

"I've never been even once." Joe said. "Isn't it strange we've lived here our whole lives and never crossed the lake?"

Why was he talking about Vermont? Something extraordinary had to have happened to cause his brother to seek him out in the middle of the week, to sniff around the camp for the fire. He waited, a slow dread casting a pall over the formerly cozy shelter.

"I like it here. Little cold for me though." Joe examined the three walls as if he had never seen a lean-to before. "Pretty quiet, that's for sure." Only the rain tampered the silence, the vast gray lake now a checkerboard in blurry motion.

Sitting on his hands, Steve studied his denim jeans fading to dirty white at the knees, hems black with soil, waiting patiently for Joe to announce the reason for his visit. Eyes closed, he remembered how he had slept with one of the campers here all last summer, in her expensive down bag that smelled of the dry cleaner. She was a grown-up sixteen-year-old from New York City who made Steve feel both old and naive at the same time. On the pill since she was thirteen, the girl touched Steve in an expert but detached fashion, as if he were an experiment under study, an experience she would talk about later to her friends in Manhattan. He hadn't cared much, though, because he hadn't had sex since Carol Ann had left him so cruelly so many years ago, denouncing him as a miser—with his emotions and his words—calling him a selfish man she had had it up to here with! (drawing an imaginary line above her considerable height). She claimed she would lose her mind if she had to spend one more winter with someone who wouldn't talk to her. She left him in November of 1975, when it snowed heavily and often, the whiteness of it blinding, the mass of it blanketing the cabin, piling up to the eaves, so that when he looked out the window he saw only white, and no light entered. Carol Ann couldn't bear the isolation of the camp as she got older, but Steve preferred it, especially in his solitary state, to being with other people.

When Joe removed his pack of cigarettes from beneath the

raincoat, Steve cleared his throat again. "Not in here, okay?"

"Sorry. I forgot. You still running every day?"

"No. Not anymore."

"God. Everything kind of stands still out here. I can see why you like it." Rain dripped on Joe's bare head, matting the short, curly hair to his pale forehead. "I bet nothing really bad happens out here. Maybe termites or something." He made a laughing noise.

Steve understood Joe was speaking about his dead child, and feared, for a moment, something had happened to the other one.

"What's going on, Joe?"

"Vernon's dead."

Steve still heard the rain, as before, beating on the tin roof, still observed his brother's figure at the edge of the lean-to, his cheeks drenched, face uplifted in an uncertain expression, and everything was exactly as it had been a second before, but a heaviness had lifted, a dark clod of weight magically levitated from Steve's bony shoulders as he walked out into the rain, his face held up to the falling sky, his eyes smarting at the contact of fresh and salt.

Zoe Mae and Charlayne slept, entangled, in a mass of sheets, discarded clothing, and fast-food wrappers. Their motel was far from port on a busy suburban road of gleaming neon and fluorescent signs. They brought their plastic- and Styrofoam-wrapped meals to their room, where they were holing up for the four days' leave, ignoring the curious stares of the desk clerk and the leering husband next door. Zoe Mae had found comfort in the strength of Charlayne's body, anchored in the safe bay of her arms. It was their third day, and they napped, blissfully, naked most of the afternoon. Zoe Mae was dreaming of her beloved grandmother when someone pounded on the door. Terrified, she leaped out of bed and charged for the bathroom, grabbing jeans and sneakers from the floor, fearing arrest, disclosure, violence, aware that in the state of Mississippi they might be put on trial for their love, which was miscegenetic and homosexual and wrong by every Bible standard.

"Zoe Mae, get your body back in here." Charlayne's voice sounded more irritated than frightened. She did not scare easily, which was one of the qualities Zoe Mae admired so. "It's only Jean. You got an emergency call just now. You're supposed to phone your mother right away."

Wearing only a pair of jeans and one tennis shoe, Zoe Mae flew out of the bathroom, adrenaline coursing, and dove for the phone beside the bed.

Her eyes constantly on Charlayne, who was pacing the room in a large man's undershirt, Zoe Mae dialed the operator to place a collect call, during which she made a bargain with God: let it not be her mother, let Dean be okay, Steve unharmed, the twins spared, and she would do what God wanted. She would give up Charlayne. Charlayne was smoking now, and Zoe Mae could tell from the way she inhaled and exhaled rapidly, not bothering to remove the cigarette, that she shared Zoe Mae's anxiety.

The operator announced the call. "Will you accept the charges, Sir?"

"Yes, Ma'am." It was Dean, and she sighed with relief to hear his voice.

"Dean! You're okay. What's happened? Is Mom all right?"

"Everything's all right, little one. We're all okay." His voice was so subdued he sounded as if he were drugged.

"Jesus! If you're all okay, why'd you scare me half to death with that message?" Zoe Mae felt angry that she had been tricked into her guilty pact with God. She cursed herself for being a coward.

"It's Vernon."

"Vernon," she echoed. She'd forgotten about Vernon. "What'd he die of?"

"Heart failure."

Zoe Mae almost laughed at the irony, but asked instead, "Where?"

"A V.A. hospital in the state of Washington." Dean's words remained a monotone, relaying the information in what she felt was a falsely passionless voice.

"So, now what happens?"

"The body's being flown back here. We're trying to put a funeral together for tomorrow or the next day, depending on when you can get back here. Will they let you go for a couple days?"

Zoe Mae grabbed a pencil and wrote FUNERAL on the margin of yesterday's newspaper, which lay on the floor, open to the crossword puzzle. "Yeah, I can try and get on a plane tonight if there's a direct flight to Montreal or something." Zoe Mae shuddered at the thought of flying, airports, renting cars; she did not want to go. She did not want to bring Charlayne and confront her family with her secret life at the moment of her father's funeral.

"I'm already one step ahead of you, Zoe Mae." Dean's voice lifted slightly, revealing a hint of his usual banter.

Dean, ever in charge, ever competent, had already reserved her a seat on a flight leaving New Orleans in three hours which would, after two changes, deposit her in Burlington, Vermont, just before midnight, where he would be waiting. He told her to have a shot of bourbon before boarding; this would fix her nervousness, he assured her, though he had never been on a plane himself. She hung up.

"Zoe Mae, those green seaweed eyes give you straight away. You're not taking me. You don't want me to come."

"He got me a ticket already," Zoe Mae pleaded. "It's reserved."

Charlayne pulled on her jeans after stubbing out her cigarette in the foil ashtray. "I'm taking a walk. Gonna try and work this out in my head. Or out *of* my head. Girl, I'm sorry to hear your daddy's dead—not that he ever did anything for you—but you're going to have to choose one of these days if you're with me or without me. I can't stand this much longer." She left without bothering to shut the door, walking briskly across the oil-stained parking lot.

As Zoe Mae finished dressing, she watched her actions in the mirror as if she were watching a film, or a stranger. Her father, whom she could not remember, was now dead. It was 2 p.m. in New Orleans, and she would find herself at home in the farmhouse before she went to sleep again. These things were happening to someone else, she thought, sheathing her freckled arms in a green hooded sweatshirt, small, strong hands expertly braiding the thick red hair, her new black-rimmed aviator glasses staring back at her quizzically. "Who was he?" she asked her reflection.

Chapter Fourteen

It was the kind of March day that dawned rarely in York Ferry, the wind barely stirring the bare branches, a warm spring sun lighting on the first yellow crocuses. The temperature reached an unheard of fifty-five degrees by 10 a.m., and Minister Eldridge, who had presided over Eleanor's funeral eleven years before, and that of William Lee Pinny, an infant, prepared himself for another burial. He was an old man, eighty-two, who found too frequently he buried the young. Vernon Pinny, not yet sixty, dead of heart failure while in long self-exile from his home and family. The ways of God are not easily deciphered by man, the minister thought, as he reached for his Bible to pray for a moment in the church before heading out to the cemetery. There would be no service, as requested by the widow, only a few words at graveside.

Cathy, Dean, Jr., and Sheila arrived early at the graveyard. The children had never before explored this part of York Ferry and chafed beneath their mother's restraining arm. Finally she let them roam, pleading with them to keep their good clothes clean. Sheila, 10, and Dean, Jr., 8, played tag among the tombstones, a few of which were over two hundred years old, moss grown into the inscriptions. The most recent belonged to Billy Pinny, buried at the feet of his great-grandfather, Caleb. Settling back in the car to wait, Cathy lit a cigarette and wondered why she was there. Vernon was not her family, not anymore. It was only tangentially out of respect for Kay, who would probably appreciate her presence. She eyed the old oak presiding over the better part of the cemetery; it was lightning-scarred and half-dead, its living half lined with robins.

Driving out from the camp in a dented old pickup, Steve balanced a mug of coffee high above the dashboard, managing not to spill one drop. He wore his funeral suit, bought in 1969, which fit him poorly, cuffs and socks glaring out from beneath the navy fabric. He felt elated without knowing exactly why; since the day before when he heard the news of his father's death, a nearly hysterical desire to laugh had grown inside of him. He pictured himself as a balloon, recently unmoored from its stake, now flying erratically and fast across the cloud-studded sky. He'd have liked to wrestle with Dean as they did in high school, their love and hate for one another entangled in their sweating limbs, the thwack of their backs on the mats, the temporary satisfaction of victory or acquiescence to defeat. He looked forward to seeing Zoe Mae, whom he imagined he would pluck from the ground against her will, as he had in years past, setting her beside the sunflowers for measuring. Had she grown taller since leaving them? At five feet, she was only half as tall as some of his mother's biggest specimens, their giant, lolling heads like the sun itself raining pollen down on his sister's red hair, sprinkling her with yellow dust. He vowed to ask Kay for seeds this year to plant around his cabin.

Inside the car, Joe anxiously fed Robby a slice of toast as they waited for Fern, who was late. The Five Oaks Cemetery was only a few minutes away, but Joe couldn't resist the urge and banged the horn to summon her. Robby laughed, his butter-and-crumb-smeared hands already dirtying his new pair of pants. Joe used his handkerchief to dab at his son's face and wiped the culprit fingers and palms. He kissed Robby on the top of his head and put his arm around him, against which the boy snuggled comfortably. As the car engine warmed, the heating system jetted blasts of hot air against their faces, making them sleepy. Joe was still confused; he felt no sorrow, no joy, only a detached ambivalence about the death of his father. When Fern finally entered the car, her face red from hurrying, he pulled her chin toward him for an unexpected kiss on the lips. "It's okay," he said. "We have plenty of time."

Dean could have walked to Five Oaks from his apartment beside the depot, but he didn't want Cathy and the kids to pass him in the car. Would she stop? Would his children be ashamed to see their father, alone and tired, walking in the road? He fretted, unable to decide, and it was time to go. He didn't understand why Zoe Mae had insisted on staying in Burlington, on renting a car at the airport, but he was too preoccupied to ponder for very long. "My father, my father," he said, over and over, the words summoning his long-buried passion for the man he had known, the slender, graceful mechanic who taught him everything about cars by doing, by example. Oh, what an example Vernon had left him. Dean looked around the barren room before shutting the door on his bachelor's studio, where he spent as little time as possible. Heading for the Jeep, pressured by lateness to drive the quarter-mile after all, Dean rehearsed his plea to Cathy. All those women he had slept with were diversions, distractions from the purpose he had feared at home, the necessity of fatherhood. He was now ready to take it on, refusing to become his father. "My father, my father." His throat ached with mourning. He would give up one of his jobs, he planned to tell her. He would adapt to her working; he would control his impatience with the children. Now that they were older, he could take them fishing, as he had Zoe Mae in the early years after Vernon left. He would make up the damage he had caused. As he backed out the short driveway, a freight train rumbled by, its whistle sharp and insistent, piercing the morning.

"Paul, I'm going to leave without you if you don't get here this minute!" Kay checked her watch, the patch of fog obscuring the dial, and put it to her ear to check: it still worked, though sometimes in fits and starts. For reasons Kay didn't understand, Zoe Mae would meet them at the cemetery after driving over from Burlington. "You'll have to get there yourself, then!" She slammed the front door and rushed down the porch steps to the car. He had made them late, and now it seemed he no longer wanted to come. Against all her ingrained impulses, Kay drove away from the farmhouse, not looking to see if he had run after her. Not even Vernon could have straightened that boy out, she thought. Vernon. His seven letters were tucked inside her pocketbook, tied in thread. She was not sure why she felt compelled to bring them, yet she knew she must. In his last letter, four months before, he seemed to blame her for his absence. What absurdity! *Her* fault? She might have handled it all differently, better, perhaps, yet she refused to accept the blame. After all, she never left anyone behind. She was so angry she failed to notice the shimmering lake in her rear-view mirror, the last of the fog dissolving in the sun, and the distant flapping of a great blue heron as it rose from its nest on the boundary of the Pinny property and flew into the light.

In bed, Paul rubbed his temples and swigged from a beer he had brought in for an eye-opener. He could not make himself get dressed. His head ached and his throat was parched, and he felt entirely sober. Everything hurt. The room was too bright for March. The shades were shut, but still, a morning halo loomed about the window.

Zoe Mae and Charlayne had been up since 6 a.m., after only four fitful hours of sleep. It was too early in the season for the York Ferry, so they drove down through Vergennes, Vermont, over the bridge into Marysville, and up Route 22 to reach the funeral. Zoe Mae was driving, and Charlayne smoked incessantly while fiddling with the radio dial. Zoe Mae was waiting to feel the grief she knew she must, but she concentrated on the familiar road, slowing carefully at Elbow Curve.

And the heads of those gathered around the open grave looked up in surprise to see the rental car with Zoe Mae and a stranger pull in the cemetery gates.

Minister Eldridge stood at the head of the plot, Kay at the other end. Joe and Steve were on one side, hastily joined by Paul, who rode up on his bike as the minister began to speak. On the other side were Zoe Mae and Dean. Behind them, the second circle consisted of Cathy and Fern beside one another, surrounded by their children, and in the outer circle Averill, who stood in back of Kay, and Charlayne, who towered over Zoe Mae. Everyone had examined Charlayne and determined she must be Zoe Mae's long-time friend from the Coast Guard.

"It seems not long ago at all that we stood in this same cemetery to lay to rest Eleanor Camden, Kay's mother, the grandmother and great-grandmother of the children here, after a terrible accident allowed God to take her to Him, away from us. And just a few sad months ago, we gathered here to bury a child, William Lee Pinny, whose place was with God, not us. Under other, distressing circumstances, today we must lay to rest the body of Vernon Robert Pinny, aged fifty-six, a young man, taken from this family by illness, an occurrence—like the accident that claimed Mrs. Camden—over which we have no control. Whom, then, do we blame? Vernon Pinny had absented himself for almost twenty years from our community, yet we gladly welcome him home to be buried in the land where he was born, beside his father and mother. We must place, instead of censure and denunciation, our forgiveness in the earth along with his mortal body. Let us ask God to help us now to forgive this man, Vernon Pinny, and to forgive ourselves." The minister closed his eyes and prayed.

Everyone, including the three children, whispered "Amen" when he finished, and there was a moment of silence, broken only by a distant bird.

Kay turned back to Averill, who put his thin arms tenderly around her, pulling her fast against his breast, for she was crying. After a moment, she extricated herself from Averill's embrace and pulled Zoe Mae, who was waiting, into her arms. Zoe Mae, on seeing her mother's tears, finally, for the first time in her twenty-two years, wept for her unknown father, her weeping mother, and her own deprivation.

Steve stepped away and looked down at the coffin. His father abandoned them all, he thought, but now it was done. Kay handed Paul the parcel of letters. And they filed out toward their cars: Dean holding the hands of his children, Cathy's back to him while she talked to Fern. The twins walked ahead, together, Joe holding Robby, Paul the letters, Steve and Charlayne side by side. Kay clutched Averill's elbow, worrying about how Paul would interpret his father's letters, whether he would blame her for all that had happened. And Zoe Mae led the procession from the cemetery.

THE END